Also from Indigo Sea Press

Novels by Tony R. Lindsay

Tattletale Roadhouse and Social Club

indigoseapress.com

Lucas Lee

His Forebears & Descendants

By

Tony R. Lindsay

Sepia Books

Published by Indigo Sea Press

Winston-Salem

Sepia Books
Indigo Sea Press
302 Ricks Drive
Winston-Salem, NC 27103

Copyright 2014 by Tony R. Lindsay

First Sepia Books edition published February, 2016

Sepia Books, Moon Sailor and all production design are trademarks of Indigo Sea Press, used under license.

For information regarding bulk purchases of this book, digital purchase and special discounts, please contact the publisher at indigoseapress.com

Cover design by Stacy Castanedo

Original Illustrations by Ben Mowers

Manufactured in the United States of America

ISBN 978-1-63066-188-5

I dedicate this book to my grandchildren:

Bart Brnjac

Katie Brnjac

Maggie Brnjac

Athena Grisette

Uly Grisette

CONTENTS

Rosalyn

1858

Cleopatra

1870

Sam Westmoreland

1876

Charlie

1880

Farris Lee

1881

Lyle Henderson

1882

Preacher Poindexter

1884

Betty Lee Kilpatrick

1891

Ava Mae Davenport

1898

Willy

1899

Olin Washington

1900

Billy Ray Lee

1912

DESCENDANTS OF LUCAS LEE

Wesley Lee

1940

Rodney Lee

1950

Tyrone Lee

1954

John Thomas Lee

1955

Mack Lee

1959

Lionel Lee

1961

Jack Lee

1962

Moses Lee

1964

Carl Lee

1967

Latisha Lee Johnson

1968

Deron Lee

1974

Donald Lee

1976

INTRODUCTION

In 1948, at age six, I made a special friend. Leroy Lee was a towering, muscular, black man who made a meager living washing cars at my uncle's automotive service business. He was a mountain of a man telling stories about his days as a professional boxer to a wisp of a boy. I was enthralled.

My dad and I hung around the service station on Saturday mornings. Then Dad and two of his brothers would go to lunch at a nearby diner. I would bring a sandwich and chips in a paper bag and eat with Leroy in his battered pickup. He told me about his boxing days, and he told me about his grandmother being sold at an auction of Negros somewhere in Virginia. Her mother had been captured in Africa and shipped to a port in Rhode Island.

One Saturday morning Dad said, "Don't make a bag lunch today. You can eat with me and the boys at the diner."

"Thanks, Dad, but I like to eat with Leroy. Let me tell you about a fight he had in Louisville."

"I don't want to hear it, and I want you to eat with us and not Leroy."

"Why can't I eat with Leroy?"

"Because it doesn't look good. That's why."

I didn't press Dad for a better explanation. He was getting riled up, and I didn't want to risk making him angrier. I had no more lunches with Leroy, but I thought about him a lot. He had an infectious laugh. When he laughed everyone around him laughed, too. Leroy was interesting and pretty darn smart.

Then I thought about how Dad felt. He was my hero. But he was wrong. Wrong about Leroy. He let racial prejudice guide his decisions. Blacks were not welcome in our church, and Dad saw no

1

problem with keeping colored people "in their place." All my life I wondered how a good, righteous man such as Dad could hold such beliefs.

I wondered about how, in the days of slavery, white men and women could whip a person unmercifully on Saturday and go to church on Sunday morning and sing praises to the Lord. How in their minds did they justify their actions? How did they reconcile cruelty with piety? Were all plantation owners Devils incarnate, or were they the products of their time?

If I had been born into a wealthy Southern family in 1825, my attitude and beliefs might have been no different from my neighbors'. Perhaps I would not have permitted brutal whipping, but I would not have wanted to set free the labor force that made me rich. I would likely have found a way, in my mind, to cling to the hope of Heaven and hold on to my human property. Maybe I would have conjured up something about "protecting" the less fortunate and less capable.

I can't say what kind of a person I would have been before the War and Surrender. I like to think I would have been an abolitionist. My best guess is that I might have tried to find a middle ground. In time, I would have cast aside the middle ground and crusaded against slavery. I like to believe that is what I would have done.

I read about the "peculiar institution" that allowed men to own other men as if they were cattle and gave rise to the prejudice that exists to this day.

My reading and my imagination provided the fodder for many stories depicting the lives of people considered chattel. Those stories and the life of the indomitable Lucas Lee are collected in this book.

CAPTAIN MONTERROSO

1794

CASTELO BRANCO, PORTUGAL

I had been away from home for ten days and nights making ready for my voyage to West Africa. Captives were being held at Fort Elmina and there should be more by the time we arrived. I would have only one night at home and then be back on the docks in Lisbon for a final four days before setting sail. I would be off on a journey facing the perils of the sea and the dangers of transporting Africans.

I had been told about a Negro who tried to sell his own son. The son spoke some Portuguese. The father understood not a word. The younger man persuaded the captain that the older man was his prisoner and not his father. He convinced the captain that he could bring a dozen more men and women. They clasped the older man in irons and soon he was one of six rowing a boat out to the ship. From the shore the boy waved to his father.

Tonight I would not worry about storms and trickery. Tonight I would make love to my beautiful wife. As I made my way home, I thought: Surely this night she will relax her rule about that sheet. Every time, she holds the sheet with both hands halfway up my back. God knows that I love her, but sometimes I could kill her.

"Ricardo, my darling," my wife called from the veranda.

"My dear Maria, how have you fared?"

"Very well indeed. I must tell you about our guest who is coming tonight."

"Tonight! We are having visitors tonight?"

"Sir Ferdinand, no less, will be our guest."

"I thought we would be alone tonight."

3

"The fifth in line for the throne is coming to our home this very night. Now hurry and make yourself presentable. I must see that preparations are complete."

Maria held up her skirts and scurried though a doorway. I grumbled aloud as I stepped down from my carriage. "The fat bastard is coming to gorge himself at my table."

At dinner that evening Sir Ferdinand's devilish grin made me sick. I loathed the king's nephew. The two of us took turns subtly insulting each other. The snide remarks and double entendres passed without Maria's involvement. After dinner, whiskey was served in the library. Closing insults were exchanged, and I assured Sir Ferdinand that I did not want to continue to match wits with an unarmed man.

We bid Sir Ferdinand goodnight. A servant led him to the guest quarters. I followed Maria up the staircase and down the hall.

"Do you think he enjoyed himself?" Maria asked.

"He enjoyed himself. He ate enough for three people."

"He does have a marvelous appetite."

"I would call it a voracious appetite. The fool eats like a swine. He resembles a pig. I think it's the jowls."

"Ricardo, you should not say such things."

"He rips into food like a ravenous wolf. He has a gastronomical fortitude unparalleled in nature. I tell you the man will devour his own arm someday in his eagerness to rush another morsel into that hole in his flabby face."

"You should not speak of Sir Ferdinand's tendency to overindulge."

"Over-gorge is more accurate. He has the insatiable appetite of a shark and the capacity of a whale. He engulfs food the way a

4

fish sucks in water. No doubt he has gills behind those fleshy ears." I crossed my hands under my chin and waved my fingers like a fish's gills. "His monstrous shadow belies the diminutive brain nestled in the fat that lines the inside of his skull. His capacity for ingestion of animal and vegetable matter is phenomenal."

We arrived at her bedchamber, and I decided to say no more about Sir Gluttony.

I opened the door and Maria brushed past me. I took notice of the plunging neckline that had so enchanted our guest all evening. Maria sashayed across the room.

I felt an urge to lift her onto the bed and rip off all those petticoats. But I would have to be content to allow her to disrobe in her dressing room. I removed my clothing and slid into bed. Maria appeared at her dressing room door clad in a floor length nightgown laced up to her neck with ribbons tied in a neat bow.

"He's amazing, Ricardo. Did you see his ring?"

"Damn it, Maria, I don't want to talk about his ring, or his oversized head, or the ripples of fat that cascade everywhere."

"Ricardo, God is not happy with you."

"Dear wife, God is not happy with that swollen toad who lies in our guest quarters. He doesn't have enough spine to give form to a worm."

"God hears you."

"I pity his chamber pot. Do you suppose our facility is adequate, dear?"

"You must pray this instant. And I will pray that God will forgive the sin that has erupted from your heart."

Maria slipped onto her knees, looked heavenward, made the sign of the cross and bowed her head.

5

"Maria, for Heaven's sake."

"Now you swear! In my presence, you are swearing, Ricardo Gaspar Alfonso Monterroso."

I threw up my hands. "Oh, for Heav…I mean…

"I know what you mean. You are so interested in the desires of the flesh and foreplay of the Devil that you will not pray for God's forgiveness. But I will pray. I will pray that God will not punish you for the terrible things you've said tonight."

I picked up my robe and headed for the door. "Pray, Maria. Pray all night. But don't pray for me. Pray for old fat-ass."

***

We sailed from Lisbon on 10 August. God, in His wisdom, had led the Pope to grant Portugal the exclusive right to exploration and trade with Africa. However, the English, French, Swedes, and the damn Spaniards were known to be plying the waters toward our destination. My ship was slow by comparison. My crew carried side arms and long guns, but we were only armed with two small cannon. If we encountered a well- armed Spanish galleon, our ship would be blown apart and sink without a trace. Lost at sea. No one would ever know we had not disappeared in a storm.

God watched over us and we arrived safely on the coast of West Africa.

Part of my plan was to capture fishermen and their villages. Even without guns, the Africans fought hard and in great numbers. I abandoned the idea of taking slaves without the use of money. A better approach was to buy blacks who were already prisoners of war and the slaves of other Africans. The tribes were constantly at war. The victorious were eager to sell us their defeated foes. It was a sensible arrangement. We traded guns, powder and goods in exchange for unwanted prisoners. God, as always, was on the side of the victors.

My ship, although small at 100 tons, was perfect for the transport of approximately 220 slaves. I could cram another twenty to thirty on board by tight packing. But the survival rate was better in a loose pack, and we had to carry less food and water. Loose packed slaves arrived at port in better condition and fetched better prices. I heard stories of tight packed ships losing half of their cargo to fevers and such like.

The men were shackled two by two, the right wrist and ankle to the left wrist and ankle of another. We didn't bind the women and children. We kept them separate from the men.

We left Africa with 218 slaves and arrived at Rhode Island having lost only five men. When we found a dead one, we unshackled the dead from the living and threw the body overboard. All the women and children survived. But we lost two crew members to the pox.

Slaves on board my ship were the lucky ones, but they did not realize their good fortune. The Negros so hated to leave their own country, that they often leap'd out of our ships into the sea. They had a more dreadful fear of the unknown than we have of Hell, tho' in reality they live better there than as prisoners in their own country. But home is home and family is family.

We reached port and rode at anchor until the whole lot of them had been taken ashore in small boats. We lined them up like a ragtag army and marched them into town and on to market. I hired a bagpiper to draw attention to our procession. A respected broker told me that my cargo looked among the best he had ever seen. He said that the previous group had looked like skeletons raised from the grave. Tight packing does that.

I set high prices. And they were worth every escudo. The best price I got was for Bo. Her tribal name was something like Bolanile, but my men called her Bo. She was strong, healthy and pretty in an African way. And she was childing maybe three months. Men will be men. So I let them have their way with Bo.

When we got her on the block, she was sold to a gentleman named Owens as two for the price of one.

MASTER ESAU

1840

BURKE COUNTY, GEORGIA

I tried to be a good man-honest, fair, my word was gold. And there was not a better cotton farmer in Georgia. Anyone would tell you that Esau Owens understood cotton, how to grow it, how to keep the weevils away, and how to get the best prices. The Lord knows I paid a full tithe to the Baptist Church.

I heard people talking about changing the name of First Baptist to Owens Baptist while I was still alive and could enjoy the honor. But I would have none of it. First Baptist was God's house, not mine. I was a man who talked the talk and walked the walk, and Christian to the core. I never had anything bad to say about anybody, even those Lutheran folks.

My darkies had good things to say about their master. They worked only eleven hours on weekdays and a half-day on Saturday. Come noon Saturday, no slave hit a lick of work for me until Monday morning. I let the house girls make ready everything in advance for their time off.

I never had a slave whipped-not once. If ever a black man had to be punished, I had the other slaves lay shame on the poor devil. To be honest, there was the time when I had two fellows hung upside down by their feet. I swore they would hang there all day, but I had them cut down inside an hour.

I treated black women even better than the men. I never had a black woman punished in any way whatsoever. Women are slightly-built, gentle by nature, and not suited for heavy work. Bo was my favorite-the tallest negress I had ever seen, big- boned too. Her girl, Jane was not nearly as tall. Jane was only thirteen when she had Lindee. That child grew to be almost as tall as her grandmother. And Lindee's boys, Lee and Lucas, were going to be two mighty big bucks.

9

We sold slaves from time to time, but always as a family-the man, the woman, and the children— all together. That was my rule, and I never broke it unless I had to for some reason.

I've always believed God-fearing blacks will have a place in heaven in one fashion or another. Maybe they will be servants. God intended for it to be that way. But life in heaven is going to be easy for everybody. Blacks have their place in the great scheme of God.

I gave my slaves an acre of choice, hill-top land and all the material they needed to build a Praise House. Of course, they didn't actually own the property. They had no legal right to own anything. But my heart was in the right place. They built a fine one- room structure with benches aplenty and a wood-burning stove right in the center. God heard more good things coming from that Praise House than from the Baptists and Lutherans combined. Wednesday night was prayer meeting. Thursday night was time for testimonials. All day Sunday was devoted to preaching, singing, shouting, and moving with the Spirit. What a time those people had.

Saturday night was dance night for the darkies. Dancing started at sundown in an old barn they scrubbed clean. I would love to have seen those women dancing. Jiggling and wiggling the way they do natural.

But I never sneaked a peek in the barn. It didn't seem right-seemed like an intrusion. I ask you how many plantation owners give a damn about intruding into the lives of the people they own. There are not many white men like me.

Some folks said I was too good to my slaves. Bill Wilson said, "Esau's going to spoil those blacks for anybody else."

I didn't care what he said. I was the largest contributor to the Baptist church and loved by my family and slaves. Bill Wilson could go to hell.

There was only one really good man in the whole damn county, other than me, and that was Mannford. He was a Negro preacher and righteous to the core. And he was a Bible preacher. Mannford did not care for anyone's interpretation of the scripture. scripture. The preacher told it like it was. He could read a bit. Mannford learned his letters from his daughter, Ruth. The Missus had taught Ruth the alphabet so she could read some Bible and children's stories to our son. I let it go. But it could have made a lot of trouble for me-teaching a slave to read.

Ruth worked in our home. She knew how to speak to white people, how to set a table, all kinds of stuff. And Ruth was a beauty.

Ruth, at the age of fourteen, had become the constant companion of my wife, Mildred. I loved my wife and watched her wither away from consumption. She hung on to life for almost two years. Mildred would allow no one to care for her but Ruth. "Only Ruth has the dignity to carry my chamber pot and make it seem like the function of a lady. She's a sweet girl and so smart. Promise me you will give her freedom after I'm in Heaven."

I nodded that I heard her, but I didn't actually agree to grant Ruth her freedom.

Mildred died on Christmas Day. Her last breath rasped slowly as I held one hand and Ruth held the other. I placed a kiss on Mildred's forehead and pulled the sheet up over her face. I walked around the bed and reached out to Ruth. She sobbed into my shoulder. My emotions spilled over. A minute before I had lost the only woman I had ever loved, but I couldn't deny that the girl in my arms was thrilling me in a way that made me ashamed. Ruth took a seat at the end of Mildred's death bed and tried to compose herself. In spite of my guilt, I took in every inch of the lovely girl. She was a dark, ripe plum. Ruth had the deep bronze coloration of her father, soft features, lean and curvy with a tiny waist.

I had to gain control of my thoughts. From that moment on, I behaved as a gentleman. Alone in my bed at night, I thought of nothing else.

As the days passed, life in our house resumed something of the old routine. I immersed myself in the affairs of the plantation and entertaining important people from around the state.

11

Ruth was kept busy with the house and seeing that luncheons and dinners were conducted flawlessly. My male guests knew that Ruth was off-limits. I would not tolerate jokes or suggestive comments in the presence of Ruth. Show disrespect to Ruth, and I would show you the door.

Two years went by and Ruth blossomed from a lovely child into an elegant young woman. I was enchanted with the preacher's daughter. Her clothes were no longer hand- me-downs, but new, even frilly, frocks that I ordered from England.

Ruth regarded me as her Master, a kindly Master to be sure, but still I owned her body. Her love belonged to her father, her mind to herself, and her soul to God.

I made known my interest in little ways such as when I boosted her onto a buckboard. Ruth fended off every foray. As time went by, I felt I would lose my mind. Damn, how I wanted her. How I wanted to get a look under all those petticoats. My desire was something akin to love.

I could order her into my bed. I considered the prospect, but I just couldn't do it. There had to be a solution, an honorable solution, and I had to find it.

"Ruth" I said, "I know your father is getting older and his back gives him a lot of misery."

"Yes, I worry and pray about him every day."

"Maybe I could take him out of working in the fields. Put him in the barn where he could feed and care for the animals."

"Oh, Master, I would do anything to see Dad's life become easier. He loves horses, and he could handle work in the barn without hurting himself."

"I heard what you said about doing anything, but all I want is a little affection and touching, you know what I mean. If you will be nice to me in a special way, I will put your dad in the barn. He could do as much work as suits him. Willy will still be there to handle the heavy lifting."

Ruth thought for a minute. "Dad can't know anything about this."

I had my answer. I thought, *"When is a little negotiation not an honorable course."*

LUCAS

1864

BALDWIN COUNTY, GEORGIA

I played like I didn't hear talkin' betwixt Marsa MacTavish and a stranger. "You have a fierce reputation for efficiency, Mr. Dietrich, but I will not hire an overseer who's not a religious man."

"Yes sir, I've been a church-goin' man all my life. I know the ways of God."

"I understand you know something about running a plantation and handling slaves."

"Ah, yes sir, I was raised on a farm not twenty miles from here, down by the fork of the river. Been pushin' slaves since I was sixteen-years-old. I only got one arm thanks to them Yankees, but Eli Dietrich don't coddle no blacks, you can ask anybody."

"Can you work a hundred slaves?"

"Oh yeah, more than that. You'll see I ain't a man to be trifled with when it comes to them darkies."

"Then it's set. You'll start in the morning. I need the fields south of the creek picked clean in three days."

"Just you leave it to me, Mr. MacTavish."

"A black preacher and a white she-devil calling herself an abolitionist have been stirring up my slaves. Abolitionist is a fancy name for a Godless creature that cares not a whit for order and prosperity. The slaves will need a stern hand to keep them in line. Mr. Dietrich, you are the man to set things right."

Wilford MacTavish owned 'bout 2000 acres. We was all born on that plantation. In 1864, the War was goin' the way I hoped it would. Each month them Yankees was gettin' closer. Everybody said so.

Early next morning, Boss Dietrich sat on a stallion and led me and forty-three more men, twenty-eight women, and twelve children over the age of eight to the southern fields.

"You folks gonna be pickin' cotton come first light. One of y'all gives me a little backtalk, and I'm gonna show you sumpin'."

I already knowed that Marsa MacTavish done finished his breakfast and was gettin' ready for a meetin' at the Church. He done saddled a white mare, a job that would have been done by an old slave he called Black Jack, but we was all needed in the fields.

All they meetings began with a prayer by Preacher Bill O'Keefe.

15

I know 'cause I talked a lot with the preacher after the war. He hated slavery, but money from the plantation owners kept his church from goin' down and fed his family.

He said that his prayin' went something like this, "Lord, give us this day our daily bread. Give us the wisdom to deal with the enemy at our gate. We ask that you send calamity down on the heads of those who would destroy our righteous way of life. Let not our people live in fear but trust you for deliverance from the forces of evil. We ask these blessings in Thy name." That's what he said.

Preacher said Palmer Harrison, was the leader of the group and Harrison said they would consider ways of hidin' stuff from the Yankees as well as how to deal with the uppity attitude of the slaves. Preacher told me that Harrison said, "A few slaves are loyal and a credit to their race, but the majority of Negras are ungrateful for the blessings of Christianity and the protection of their God-fearing masters."

Preacher said heads nodded and they was a bunch of amen's. O'Keefe said that Margaret Kennedy was the onliest female at the meeting. She was Missus of Fair Oaks Plantation down by the river. Heard she operated and drinkin' and dancin' place till she married that old Kennedy fool. Weren't long till he up and died. She was a hard-drivin' woman. Accordin' to the preacher, the men listened to Kennedy. She said something like, "The slavery of Africans is a blessing to the white women of the South. My sisters are free from the drudgery of workin'. Our virtue is protected by black women who provide an outlet for the lust God done put in the pants of our men and boys."

Preacher said he couldn't believe his ears. Not a man at the table expected such nasty words to come from a lady—even a dance hall lady.

O'Keefe said he thanked Miss Kennedy for gracing the group with her presence. But Kennedy was not finished. "Boys are naturally curious and always in need of release of their seed. We all know it's true. Even our poor beasts are subject to a lad's prongin'. And Palmer Harrison, you know I speak the truth. Don't you deny it."

"You should have seen Harrison's face," said the preacher. The men lowered their heads and looked left and right, all the time grinnin'. Preacher said Margaret Kennedy was still not finished. "Thank God in His wisdom for the servitude of the African race. A pretty little mulatto is perfect for keeping our men and boys drained and in control of themselves in the company of ladies."

O'Keefe's said he most died. "Enough! Please, Miss Kennedy. We appreciate your insight into human nature but no further explanation is required."

Preached told them folks "The economic benefits of slavery are obvious, but there's a far more fundamental reason for the servitude of Negroes. As the descendants of Ham, the evil son of Noah, all black people are cursed by God."

O'Keefe said he read from the Bible. It's somewhere in Genesis.

"And Noah began to be a husbandman, and he planted a vineyard: and he drank the wine, and was drunken; and he was uncovered within his tent. And Ham, the father of Canaan, saw the nakedness of his father, and he told his two brethren without. And Shem and Japheth took a garment, and laid it upon both their shoulders and went backward, and covered the nakedness of their father; and their faces were backward, and they saw not their father's nakedness. And Noah awoke from his wine, and knew what his youngest son had done unto him. And he said, Cursed be Canaan; a servant of servants shall he be unto his brethren. And he said, Blessed be the Lord God of Shem; and Canaan shall be his servant. And God shall enlarge Japheth, and he shall dwell in the tents of Shem; and Canaan shall be his servant. And Noah lived after the flood three hundred and fifty years. And all the days of Noah were nine hundred and fifty years, and he died."

O'Keefe told them men, "There can be no doubt Noah was God's man on earth. The curse of Noah was the curse of God. The will of God condemned Ham and Canaan and their descendants to be the slaves and servants of their brethren for all generations."

The preacher said he knowed that the punishment of Ham was harsh for the sin of lookin' at his father's nakedness. But the Bible said, Noah awoke from his wine and knew what his youngest son had

17

done unto him. A much greater sin might have occurred than lookin' at his father's naked body. Regardless of what happened, the important point in God's word was that the children of Ham were turned as black as the sin Ham committed and are doomed to be slaves forever."

O'Keefe said Marsa Langford was next to talk. Langford said his words wouldn't be nice in front of Miss Kennedy, and he asked for her permission. She laughed and pounded the table with her fists.

Langford said, "I'm witness first-hand to the nature of Africans, and I know they are lewd to the core. Everybody knows black women have high, round fannies, and the men have, ah, instruments, bigger than any white fellow."

Preacher said every man at the table snapped his head toward Margaret Kennedy.

She pounded the table some more.

O'Keefe told Langford "Please, I beg you. This is the house of God. We should not speak in a way that ain't nice."

Preacher told me that he asked if anyone had an idea as to what could be done about the Yankee invasion. They all agreed that their most important things should be buried far from their plantations, but some stuff had to be left for them soldiers to find.

***

I watched as Eli Dietrich rode between rows of cotton and told us slaves to work harder. A breeze carried cotton lint and the smell of our sweat. A crow pushed off from a high branch in a cottonwood and headed toward the swamp. "Kkaaa-kkaaa."

Dietrich lashed a skinny woman in her thirties. Old Jack couldn't say nothin' no longer. He talked to Dietrich from about ten feet away. "Boss, be merciful, please, we's workin' hard as we can."

18

Dietrich looked down at Jack. "You got sumpin' else to say?"

"No suh, but we all know dem Yankees is in Milledgeville, no more than fifty miles away. We gwine to be free, boss."

My brother, Lee, yelled, "We gwine to be free!"

Dietrich showed no sign of bein' mad. He pulled a pistol from a belt around his waist and called for all work to stop. He pulled the hammer back into the cocked position and took aim.

A shot rang out through the valley and echoed off the ridges. Jack was hit in the center of his forehead. Old Jack fell like a tree onto his back and never drawed another breath.

Me and Lee stood there disbelievin' what our eyes had seen. Women sobbed. Every one of us called on God. With a wave of his pistol Dietrich said, "Jeb, tie Lee between them two trees over there." Jeb did as he was told.

"Tie him, and you better tie him tight."

***

Marsa MacTavish was comin' back from his meetin' at the church when he heard the gunshot. He galloped toward the south fields. He got close to the bank of the creek where Dietrich and us slaves were gathered. Lee screamed with each crack of the whip, "O, pray don't. No mo. O, pray don't."

Dietrich's eyes was wide open. "You think you can't stand it, but you can. I don't see as you got no option, black boy."

Blood flowed down Lee's back, butt and legs. I could see a shoulder bone. White it was.

MacTavish rode into the center of our bunch with his pistol held above his head.
"What's happening here?"

19

"We had ourselves a little insurrection, sir. Ain't nothing I can't handle."

MacTavish looked at Jack's body on the ground, eyes open.

"Don't you worry none, Mr. MacTavish," said Dietrich. "He was not much help in the field. Couldn't do hardly nothing."

MacTavish put his gun in the holster under his arm. "I'll be in my study. Come see me the minute you're finished here. Preacher O'Keefe is coming to dinner tonight, and I don't want him to know anything about this business. He's not fooling me. His heart is not with the South."

MacTavish rode at a trot to the Big House. I knowed he could hear Lee's screams.

Lee's limp body was cut down and left layin' in the sun. Mosquitoes and gnats crawled all over him.

At sundown, we carried Lee to the quarters. We sat in the dim light of two oil lamps. Lee, barely alive, had lost most of his blood. A young boy pushed through the door. "Boss Dietrich comin'! Boss says we all gwine to watch. He's gonna whip Lee some mo'."

I got on my feet and folded a wool sack over my right hand and went over to where Lee was layin' on his stomach.

Tears poured down my face, I reached under Lee's head and clamped a rag over his nose and mouth. I looked away. I held the rag until Lee's breathin' stopped. "Tell Boss Dietrich there ain't no use to whip Lee no mo'. He's dead."

We moved Lee's body to a shed and covered it with sacs. The next day we would have a service and bury him after sundown.

Around midnight, my mother, Lindee, crept to where I was layin' on my back. "Son, I'm yo momma, and I love you with all my heart. And you know how much I loved Lee. I loves all my chillin. I want you to have sumpin'."

"What is it, Momma?"

From under her shawl, Momma lifted a small handgun with two short barrels. "Aunt Jane took it from old Massa Crane's house when he died. It's got two bullets, but if you use it to end your own life, you will only need one pull of the trigger. I don't ever want to see you suffer da way Lee done. If you is ever faced with a whippin' that's gonna kill you, promise me to end yo life quick and without pain. Promise me dat."

"I will, Momma. I promise."

I took the pistol and put it under my sleepin' mat. Later, I heard a noise at the back door of our shack—three taps and a scratching sound. It meant a slave was askin' to come in. I opened the door to Jeff, a boy from the Ball Plantation. Jeff's face shined. "Lucas, I got good news. Dem Yankees is way past Milledgeville. Dey ain't no mo' than twenty miles from here. Dey be here by sundown tomorrow."

I begun to think hard, but I didn't say nothing. "Ain't you happy? Why ain't you sayin' nothing?"

I shook Jeffs hand and nodded thanks for taking the risk to bring good news to us. "You better get back."

Jeff run out the door.

We was pickin' cotton at sunup. Boss Dietrich ridied through long white lines of cotton. He laughed as we peed without leaving our places. Women squatted with their dresses fanned out around them. Mens had no privacy at all.

I had not slept all night. I had trouble stayin' on my feet as Dietrich came up to me. "What's matter, boy? You want some of what your brother got? I ain't a man of mercy. You ought to know that by now. And Master MacTavish ain't no man of mercy. You best know that, too."

Dietrich cracked his whip across my back. I cried out. He curled the whip across his lap. He turned in his saddle to look down at me. I put up my right hand. It was wrapped in a rag.

My hand was an inch from Dietrich's chin. "Lucas, what in hell are you doing? You ain't supposed to come near me. I'm gonna strip the hide off your black ass. You hear me, boy?"

I pushed my hand into Dietrich's face. Then, I pulled the trigger.

The bullet hit him in the mouth knocking out some teeth and went on into the back of his throat. He fell from his horse and thrashed on the ground like a chicken without a head.

I watched with ease of mind like I never felt before. Dietrich grabbed his throat and rolled over and over in the dirt. He tried to stand. Then he fell out on the ground.

All of us gathered around to watch.

What would happen next? Would we all be punished because of what I had done?

I told them to be quiet. I called a young girl to me. "Go tell Marsa dat Boss done been thrown from his horse. He's hurt bad, and he's callin' for the Marsa."

She took off to the Big House.

I told them no harm would come to 'em. The Yankees would be on the plantation by sundown. I told them to go back to pickin' cotton.

"Momma, you act like you is tending to Boss. Leave de rest up to me."

She told me to save the other bullet to end my life in case the Yankees didn't come in time to keep the whites from killin' us.

"Trust me, Momma. And trust God."

Dietrich was losin' his battle to stay alive. He stopped

22

strugglin' and looked me in the eyes. He tried to say something. Blood sprayed from his mouth. I rolled him onto his belly.

We all looked up as Marsa rode up and quick dismounted. His pistol drawn.

"Over here, Marsa."

Me and Momma acted like we was worried about Boss Dietrich. MacTavish told us to stand back. He knelt over Dietrich and rolled him onto his back.

I jammed the pistol against the back of the Marsa's neck. I pulled the trigger.

MacTavish jerked as the bullet dug into him. The old sumbitch didn't have long.

I shoved their heads together, face up, ear against ear. Their big eyes glared up at me. My face in their faces.

I chewed my words and spit 'em out. "By God, I ain't a man of mercy, either."

LINDEE

1864

BALDWIN COUNTY, GEORGIA

Lucas and me and the rest of us watched as Marsa and Boss choked on they own blood. We was all grinnin'.

Oley said, "Lucas, what we gonna do? White folks will skin us alive if they find out we kilt them two."

Lucas said, "They ain't gonna find out. Me and you are de only ones will ever know what we do with de bodies of dem two bastards. We gonna tell dem white folks dat the old bachelor sumbitch and Boss left in a wagon this morning. I hear that a lot of white people be leavin' afore de Yanks come."

"Tell me what to do."

"First we get dem two in da cotton wagon and move 'em to de woods behind our cabin."

I trailed along as Lucas and Oley hauled the bodies to a lane leading to our cemetery south of the Quarters. Lucas told Oley, "Build us a good pine box for Lee."

"What 'bout dese two?"

"We ain't gonna need but one box."

Lucas wouldn't let me see what they was doin' but he told me about it later.

Lucas began diggin' in the graveyard. By the time Oley finished the coffin and placed my boy's body inside, Lucas had a grave 'bout seven feet deep.

"Oley, we gonna put dem mulifuckers in the bottom of dat

hole. We'll bury Lee on top of 'em. I think Lee would like that."

"Yeah, dat way there ain't no graves of Boss and Marsa for dem Yankees or any white folks to find. Let's do it."

Two bodies thudded face-down onto the bottom of the grave and were covered by two feet of dirt. Then Oley and Lucas lowered the coffin. They finished filling the grave and smoothed a mound. Oley made a wooden cross and pushed it into the dirt.

Near sundown, Lucas took all of us to Lee's restin' place.

Tim kinda read scripture from an old Bible. He turned pages. "The Lord's my shepherd, and in Heaven, we ain't gonna want for nothing. There ain't gonna be no evil men to hurt us when we's walkin' by the water. There's gonna be goodness and mercy and it will last forever. Amen."

Tim closed the Bible and looked up toward the sky. "Lord, take our brother, Lee, and be real good to him. And Lord, don't let the white men kill us for what we done. Amen."

Lucas got us close to him. "I done took care of de bodies of Marsa and Boss. Ain't nobody ever gonna find 'em. Dem Yankees gonna be here tonight or in the momin'. Everybody gotta tell 'em that Marsa and Boss was scared of Yankees and dey left in a wagon going south on the old road. Say no mo. You hear? Say no mo. Tell 'em that y'all didn't see 'em leave, but everybody said dey done left. Yankees is here to help us, but we can't trust 'em 'cause dere skins is white."

***

Before sunrise the next morning, our mens herded nine cows, four goats, two calves, and twelve pigs through the woods and way back in the swamp. The animals were put inside a pen formed in a most-like circle against the deeper water of the swamp. The mens buried barrels of grain, corn and potatoes and covered over so nobody could tell what they did.

Near mid-day, we seen the first sign of Yankees. A cloud of dust above the trees about a mile up the road. We laughed and hugged and gathered to welcome the soldiers but then we got scared. Bunches of dirty, worn-out, mean-looking men come past. Some of 'em spit at us.

We stood real quiet with Lucas out front. Yankees sorta marched toward the Big House tramplin' everything flat. An officer rode up to Lucas. "Where's your master?"

"He ain't here no mo."

"I'll tell you what, boy. You better tell me where the hell he's at right now."

"Him and Boss rode off in a wagon yestiddy. They went down de road yonder."

"Yeah, right. And I'm a circus clown, and Thunder here is a buffalo. My men are hungry. You better tell me straightaway where we can find some grub or I'm gonna grab that pickaninny there, and stick my hand down her throat. Then I'm gonna yank her inside-out like a sock."

I was about to cry but Lucas held up his hand to me. "Dere's ham and bacon in de smokehouse, cows over in dat field, and a lot of chickens. Dere's pigs, too. I heard Massa got some stuff in de house, but I ain't never seen it."

The Yankee didn't say nothin'. He looked at all of us like he was studyin' something. Finally, he said to Lucas, "You get that damn bunch and get 'em in those shacks and stay there. You hear me?"

"Yes, Marsa."

The Yankee and Lucas looked each other eye to eye. Right then, that Yankee knowed Lucas weren't scared of no man.

The Yankee rode off. Lucas hurried us into our cabins.

We huddled up together. So far, no hurt had come to us, but

them Yankees was actin' more like a bunch of thieves than a army gonna give us freedom. We listened to the Big House bein' tom apart. Every animal was kilt or led away.

A bunch of soldiers headed into the woods in the direction where Oley and the others had hid the animals and food barrels.

I said to Oley, "If dey finds dem animals and dat other stuff, we is finished."

"They ain't gonna find nothing. Dem Yankees ain't goin' very far into dat swamp. Dey don't know it like we does."

Lucas said he was goin' to the Big House to talk with the Yankees. I begged him, "Don't do it, son. He told us to stay here. They'll kill you sure."

"Momma, iffin dey don't leave us sumpin, we's gonna die anyway."

"I'm yo momma, and I'm goin' with you. Final."

A big soldier holding a crystal glass about a quarter full of liquor met us on the steps of the porch.

"What you want, boy?"

"I gotta talk to de man."

An officer come struttin' out and wrinkled his nose at Lucas. With one hand on his pistol and the other hand on the handle of his sword, he come to the edge of the porch and spat tobacco juice at Lucas' knees. "Thought I told you to stay in them damn shacks. Guess you want to die right here and right now."

"No, suh, I just wants to ax you to leave us a little sumpin, so we don't starve when you is gone, suh."

"Look here, boy, I don't give a damn about darkies. I just want this business over and done, so I can get back to Pennsylvania. You can all go to hell for all I care. Anyway, a district man will be here in a day or two. He'll see to the likes of you. Now get back in that shanty, before I change my mind about shooting your black ass."

"Yes, suh."

Me and Lucas ran to the quarters.

Mid-afternoon, the bunch came out of the woods without any animals or barrels.

The next morning the Yankees sat the Big House and the main barn on fire. Then they strung together long lines of men and wagons. The last Yankee marched off the plantation in a downpour rain.

Flames burnt up the barn, but about half of the Big House was still standin'. We was a happy bunch. We danced and sung after them bluecoats were gone. "Oley, go fetch dem animals. We don't want 'em to die in dat swamp," Lucas said.

The mens sat out through the woods. They come back with the barrels but missing one calf and one pig.

"Sorry 'bout dat, Lucas, We lost a calf and a pig. Dey drown in de swamp."

"What? Couldn't you find de bodies of dem beasts?"

Oley said, "Got 'em right here. We's gonna have ourselves a feast!"

From the edge of the woods, Oley pulled the bodies of a pig and a calf. We washed, butchered, and skewered 'em over a roarin' fire. We feasted on shoulder roast, rump roast, and pork.

Our bellies was full and the Yankees were gone. Marsa and Boss were rottin' wherever Lucas put 'em. We went through the ashes of the big house looking for anything we could use. The Yankees had smashed most everything they didn't carry off or set on fire. I was using a broomstick to dig around when I found a burnt oak box as big as a pumpkin. The box had packs of real store-bought tea. Under the tea, I found a tea set like the white folks sip. I lifted it for all to see. That night, the silver stuff sat in the center of the table in my cabin.

The mornin' after the Yankees marched off, Lucas gathered us together. "White men will be comin' around here sooner or later. Dey will want to know where is Marsa MacTavish and Boss Dietrich. The local folk won't never believe dey left in a wagon.

We got to have a better story about why dey ain't here. Ain't but one story good enough— Yankees kilt 'em. We gotta say dere was a fight with words on de porch of de Big House 'tween dem Yankees and Massa and Boss. Massa got real mad. Boss too. Dem Yankees shot 'em both and took dere bodies with 'em. You say Lucas heard de Yankee leader say he didn't want nobody to ax no questions and cause no trouble. Tell 'em Lucas heard de Yankees say dey was gonna bury Marsa and Boss where dey would never be found. Dat's all we knows. Say no mo."

Lucas asked us includin' the chillin, to say the story 'bout what happened to Marsa and Boss.

"Yankees kilt' em."

"Did ya see de Yankees kill 'em?"

"No, but Lucas seen it."

Lucas poured a quart of pig's blood on the porch and down the steps of the Big House.

Some days later a white man driving a buckboard bumped onto the farm and pulled up beside me and Lucas.

"Where is Master MacTavish?"

"Yankees kilt Marsa. Seen it myself. Dey kilt Boss, too. Yanks took dem dead bodies and all kinds of stuff with 'em. Went yonder way."

"Step closer to me, boy. I said closer, damn you. Now look me straight in the eye and listen to what I'm going to tell you. Wilford

MacTavish and I own a schooner. You lie to me and I'll ship your black ass in chains to work in a salt mine in Louisiana. It's a bad way to die. The salt eats away your flesh but it takes a long time. And then your soul will burn in hell for the sin of lying. Do you believe that?"

"Yes, suh."

"Let me see your eyes and answer me this question. Are you sure Wilford MacTavish is dead?"

"Massa is dead. He's sho nuf dead."

The man took a rag from his pocket and wiped his forehead. He didn't say no more. He turned the buckboard around and drove away.

More days passed with no whites. Then, 'bout noon, a rider come down the road from Milledgeville. I kept on workin'. Lucas put his hoe down and moved up to meet the stranger. The man smiled as he got off his horse and put out his arm to shake hands with Lucas—the first time any white man ever done that.

"My name is George Howard. I'm a Union man, but my fighting days are over. These days, I'm the District Man for the Bureau of Refugees, Freedmen, and Abandoned Lands, or if you prefer, the Freedmen's Bureau."

Lucas didn't say nothin'.

"And you are?"

"I'm called Lucas."

"Do you have a last name, Lucas?"

"I don't reckon so."

"Interesting isn't it? I have two first names and you don't have a last name," Lucas didn't say nothin'. Howard cleared his throat.

"Well, Lucas, the war will soon be officially over and you're going to need to get used to being a free man. But, now, I need to talk to Mr. Wilford MacTavish. Can you take me to him?"

"No suh, Marsa's dead. Boss too."

"What happened?"

"Yankees kilt 'em."

"Please, tell me about it."

Lucas told Howard that Marsa and Boss got to arguing with the Yankees. The Yankees shot 'em both right there on the porch. The Yankees took the bodies with them so there wouldn't be no questions.

"I see, Lucas. So it's just you and the other Negros here?"

"Yes suh."

"Well, I will need to confirm the deaths of Mr. MacTavish and the other fellow. Then I'll try to be of some assistance to you. When the war ends in a few days, I'll be the representative of the military court for this district. In effect, I will be the law. Do you understand?"

Lucas nodded.

"I'm going to be here for a few days. Is there a room somewhere I can use for a headquarters?"

Lucas pointed toward the Big House. "Most of de place is done burned, but dere some rooms fit for stayin'."

"That will be fine. I will need to talk more with you later."

***

Howard spoke with us one at a time. His questions always ended with, "What happened to Mr. MacTavish and the other man?"

31

"Yankees kilt 'em. Lucas seen it."

It all sounded the same, even to me.

I think Howard made a plan right then to find out what really happened to them two.

Howard asked to see five-year-old Kate. She was always a talker. When she went to see Howard, she took with her a doll made out of a corncob and rags.

Kate told me that Howard asked, "What's your doll's name?"

"Her name's Kate, same as mine."

"Well, Kate, I want to show you something."

Howard reached into the box and pulled out a store-bought doll in a green outfit and matchin' bonnet. Kate told me that her mouth dropped open. Howard told Kate that he was gonna give the doll to his little girl when he got back to Tennessee.

"She's so pretty!"

"How would you like this doll for your very own?" Kate could not say a word.

"This can be your doll. I will give it to you, but first you have to do something for me."

"What you want?"

"Just tell me the truth. Your mamma told you to always tell the truth. Right?"

"Uh huh."
"Then tell me the truth about what happened to Master and Boss, and the doll will be yours."

Kate said she never took her eyes off the doll. "I'll tell ya, but ya can't tell nobody."

"Go on."

"Lucas kilt 'em."

Howard took a deep breath and didn't say nothin' for a minute. "Can you tell me why he killed them?"

"Cause dey kilt old Jack, and dey whipped Lee most dead. We all had to watch."

"I see. And what did Lucas do with the bodies after he killed those men?"

"Don't know, don't nobody know."

"Thank you, Kate. You are a good girl. Here's your doll."

Kate said she skipped to the door. She looked back at Howard. "I'm gonna name her Kate."

I told Lucas what I heard from Kate.

Lucas' shoulders slumped. "Tell Kate I need to see her."

"Kate, tell me 'bout your new doll."

"Mr. Howard done give it to me."

"Did he ax you some questions?"

"Uh huh, but I didn't tell him nothin'."

"Kate, you gotta tell me de truth. I gotta know. Did you tell Mr. Howard that I kilt Marsa and Boss?"

"Uh huh, but he ain't gonna tell nobody."

Lucas said he could only whisper, "That's all, Kate. Go play with your doll."

The next morning Howard called for Lucas to come to the room where he had made his office. "Lucas, I know what happened to Mr. MacTavish and that Mr. Dietrich."

"Yes, suh."

"I have to explain something to you, Lucas. I'm the law here, and I have to do what is right. I swore I would uphold the law, and I take my oath seriously."

"Yes, suh."

"Hear me out, Lucas. I'm not saying what you did to those two men is not the justice they deserved. But justice is not for me to decide. I must uphold the law and someone in Milledgeville, the District Judge, will decide what is justice in your case."

"I know in my heart you's a good man. You will do what is right in the eyes of God."

"Go back to your chores, Lucas. We'll talk again."

The next morning Howard put in writin' his report to the judge. He heard a noise comin' from outside his office. Howard got up from his chair and walked to a window. On the lawn several chillin was all around Lucas.

The biggest boy hung on to Lucas' left leg and yelled for the other boys and girls to help him. "We got him! Come on, we got him."

With lots of shoutin' and laughin', the chillin pulled at Lucas trying to drag him to the ground. Lucas held up till he fell on his back. There was more whoopin' and laughin'. Lucas' own chillin piled on and called for him to "give up."

Lucas easy tossed them kids away. More of them joined the fun, but Lucas wouldn't give up.

Bell was nine-years-old, but no bigger than a five-year-old. She had a bad leg and walked with a stick crutch. Bell laughed as the other kids tried to keep Lucas down. A boy yelled, "Come on, Bell, you got to help us."

Bell threw her stick down. She landed right on Lucas' chest. It was the last straw.

"I give up! I give up!"

A roar went up from the chillin. They had bested the big man, no doubt about it.

Bell got back on her feet and tucked the crutch under her arm. Chillin swarmed all over her.

Howard had seen enough. It was time to do what had to be done. "Lucas, I want to see you."

"Yes, suh."

"Now, Lucas. This instant."

Howard was seated behind his desk when Lucas came in the room. "Lucas, I explained how the law and justice work, and I told you about the oath I took to uphold the law. I'm sending this report to the District Judge today."

Howard turned the paper and shoved it to the edge of the desk in front of Lucas.

"There, you can read it for yourself." Lucas didn't say nothin.

"Then I will read it for you, Mr. Lucas."

Howard paused for a moment as the corners of his mouth turned up. "This report says—Yankees kilt 'em."

GEORGE HOWARD

1866

BALDWIN COUNTY, GEORGIA

Before leaving Lippincott Plantation in the winter of 1865, I had assured Lucas of forty acres and a mule that the federal government promised to displaced persons living on abandoned lands.

Smiling faces greeted me when I drove onto the old farm on a buckboard in the spring of 1866. I brought with me a fancy new toy wagon to be shared by all the children and seven crates stuffed with forty hens and a young rooster. I knew the Yankees had eaten or stolen every chicken on the farm.

Tears welled in Lucas' eyes as he looked over the flock of birds. Lucas reached for my hand and engulfed it with both of his huge hands.

I said, "Lucas, let's get down to business. There will be a fellow from Milledgeville here in the morning with some important documents. I'm here to represent the Bureau and see that you get what is rightly yours."

"Are we really gonna get forty acres and a mule?'

"I'm sure of it. But we should be able to do better. The government says that each displaced family must get the means to stay alive. You've got about six families here, right?"

"Yes, suh."

"By my reckoning, each family should each get forty acres and a mule." Lucas smiled.

"You let me worry about it, Lucas."

Mid-morning the following day, a horse with rider trotted onto the farm. The man dismounted and gave a perfunctory shake of my hand. He nodded toward Lucas. "I'm Thaddeus Perdue, District Surveyor and Recorder of Deeds. I know who you are, Mr. Howard, and this must be Lucas. You're kind of famous in these parts, boy. They say you are not a man to be trucked with. Folks around here still don't believe them Yankees killed Wilford MacTavish and that overseer fellow."

I ignored the comment and asked, "What's the first step?"

"I've got a map and some information here, and I'm going to need a little time to look around. I see here you've got some mules."

I looked to Lucas for a response. "Yes suh. We got three mules. Hid 'em from the Yankees."

"Only three mules?"

"Yes. Suh. Three-and 01' Ben, but he's 'bout dead."

"Really, that's too bad, now ain't it?"

Right away, I knew we were going to have a problem with Thaddeus Perdue. I cleared my throat. "Mr. Perdue, there is something else we need to discuss. I'm sure it will not be a problem."

"What's that?"

"Six families live on this land and according to our government each family is due forty acres and a mule."

"It ain't gonna happen, Mr. Howard. These darkies ain't nothing but one big family. Forty acres. That's all they're gonna get."

Lucas took a step closer to Perdue. "Me and Ester been married a long time. The same with Bill and Maggie, and the same with Coy and Anna."

"Is that so? Married, are you? Who performed the ceremony, some preacher blacker than midnight?"

"No. He was white. Ordained and all by the Church."

"You got a name for this preacher?"

"His name was Preacher Ridgeway."

"Joshua Ridgeway?"

"Yes suh. That's him all right. He can tell you that we's six married families."

"That's gonna take some doing, boy. Joshua Ridgeway was killed last year, shot in the gut by one of your damn Yankee friends. They say it took him three days to die. He prayed the whole time when he weren't crying. I don't know why God would

38

let a white man suffer that way. And him a preacher to boot. Guess we'll understand it all by and by." Perdue's face twisted into a smirk. "Boy, I'm gonna ask you a question. Was there anything written down somewhere about these so-called marriages?"

"No, suh. Not that I knows of." Perdue grinned. He glanced at me.

"That's not fair, Perdue, and you know it."

"I told you it ain't gonna happen. Forty acres, no more. Oh, yeah, and one mule. The rest of this plantation and three mules are going to be part of Mr. MacTavish's estate."

Perdue mounted his horse and turned to look down at Lucas and me. "At seven in the morning, we'll finish this business. You will need a last name, boy. I reckon you're gonna be Lucas MacTavish."

Lucas spat on the ground. "I ain't gonna be Lucas MacTavish."

"Then you better get a last name. I ain't recording no deed without a family name."

I started to object, but Perdue urged his horse forward and galloped toward the Big House.

I'm a religious man and unaccustomed to swearing. But I roared, "Stupid, stinking, snake bastard!"

"That's alright," Lucas said. "It won't help none to get mad."

"Lucas, don't you know what he's going to do? He's will deed to you the worst forty acres on the plantation, probably that swamp, and a dying old mule. The worst part is there won't be anything I can do about it as long as he stays within the law."

"I know I'm gonna get that swamp. I've already thought about it."

"You have?"

"Yes, suh. But there ain't more than twenty acres of swamp, and we'll still have twenty acres to plant crops, pen our cows and pigs, and raise our chickens. There's sumpin' else. That swamp goes right down to the high bank at the edge of the river. We can dig a trench through that mound and drain most of the swamp. And swamp bottom makes mighty rich soil."

"By heaven, Lucas, I think you're right. But you're going to need a mule, a strong mule."

Lucas looked down at his feet. "I thought 'bout that, too. But you got to let me do the worryin'."

I asked, "You got any idea about a family name? You will need one in the morning."

"I got to think 'bout it."

Lucas gazed around at the rolling hills and green pastures dotted with giant oaks and spreading maples. Then his attention focused on the old slave cemetery.

I said, "If you wouldn't mind having a first name for a last name, I would be honored if you chose 'Howard' for a family name."

"It's a name I ain't ever gonna forget, and I'll do it iffin that's what you want."

"It's not what I want that matters. It's what you want."

Lucas was silent for a moment. "If it won't hurt your feelings none, I'm gonna choose another name."

"No problem at all. I can see that you've made a decision."

"Yes, suh. I done made up my mind. My brother Lee is buried over there. He was a good man, a better man than me. My name's gonna be Lucas Lee. We gonna be the Lee Family."

I started to hug Lucas but it didn't seem right. He continued, "I been thinkin' a lot 'bout that mule we gotta have. We has to have a mule if we's gonna make a farm.

"That's true."

"If Ol' Ben was to die tonight, that surveyor fellow would have to let us have one of them young, strong mules. Right?'

"Yes, he has to give you a mule. It's the law."

I followed as Lucas entered the shed where Ben was standing on three legs and dangling the fourth. The mule was hardly able to raise his head.

Lucas stroked Ben's neck as he must have done a thousand times. "Ben, you ain't gonna believe this, but I'm a free man. You heard it right-a free man. Listen up, Ben, tomorrow I'm gonna be Mr. Lucas Lee."

Lucas asked Ben if he liked the name. The mule made no objection. I could tell Lucas was thinking about the long days he and Ben had spent plowing fields and hauling cotton. Lucas told me that many times when the ground was dry and hard, he had pushed the plow as Ben strained to pull it. Lucas said he always talked to Ben as they worked together. The mule had seemed to understand what was on Lucas' mind and in his heart.

I stood silently as Lucas pulled a hog-bleeding knife from a wooden box. He got on his knees and looked toward heaven. "Ben, Mr. Howard, we gonna pray now."

God, you must need a mule to plow them fields in heaven. Ol' Ben is the finest mule you 's ever gonna get. He ain't never hurt nobody, never tried to kick or bite. Ben's plowed many an acre and toted some heavy loads. He's the best mule on earth. He'll be the bestest in heaven. God, you know I love Ben, and you gonna love him too. Please forgive me for what I got to do. Ben is gwine to heaven, and if I get there too, me and Ben is gonna do some plowing for you.

Amen.

41

Vignettes of Years in Slavery

LOUISA

1848

EDEN, GEORGIA

"Be careful with that plow! Damn your black ass anyway. You've done hurt that sucklin' in your belly sure as hell. I might just give you a whippin' you ain't never gonna forget."

"Baby's fine, Boss. Didn't hurt one bit. Plow done hit a root and mule backed up. I be careful sho' nuf."

I took a few seconds to run my hand across my belly. "You be fine, baby. You ain't hurt. Please don't be hurt."

Under my breath, I said, "You be careful, too, mule." Then I snapped the reins. "Yep, Yep."

We planted potatoes and beets, then pumpkins and carrots for the hogs. I wore a straw hat and a cotton dress with nary underneath. Tried to keep my dress down decent, but it hung over my belly hump and lifted up to my knees.

I plowed till quitting time. Boss didn't make women work a full day during the last days before the baby come.

I waddled along to a fork in the farm road. The right fork led down to the quarters, the left to a big white house. I started to turn right.

"You ain't goin' to the quarters, girl. Get along up to Master's house and wait for me."

I begun to shake all over. Couldn't catch my breath. Then I headed up the left fork.

At sundown, Boss rode up to the porch where I's still shiverin'. He was followed by eight womens and kids, hoes in hand. Boss told a girl to scoop out a pit about the size of a wheelbarrow in the sand ground. All the women began to sob and lean on each another.

I got face down with my big belly in the pit and my back level to the ground. The women cried pitiful as lashes dug into me.

I screamed, "No more, please God, no more."

LODDIE

1849

CRAWFORD COUNTY, GEORGIA

"Get yourself down to the quarters. Then you can cry and carry on all you want. But I don't want to hear it. My health is not good and the doctor says I should not let anything upset me. The Master does not want me upset either."

Missus did not allow carrying on when a child was sold.

44

Missus said, "Dottie is about eight and you've known all along that we were going to sell her when she was big enough to be useful and we could get a good price. We sell yearlings every year and I don't hear any cows bubbling and making a fuss. Dottie is gone and you better get used to it."

Sometimes I wish I was God.

If I was God, I would sell Missus' precious Timmy. That's what I'd do. I'd turn him black and sell him to a buyer from Louisiana. Then I'd watch from Heaven while Missus yelled, cried, and carried on most miserable.

I dreamed about it. I dreamed I was God. I listened to Missus moan and babble. Then I told her that the cows don't even raise their heads when a yearling is sold. I swear I would do it if I was God.

Down in my cabin I cried my heart out. Dottie was so sweet, so happy. I knowed that someday she would be sold, but she didn't know it. That's all I could give her—eight years of happy.

When she went to market, I bet she was sold to a good man. Maybe in Virginia. She could work in a Big House. She's smart and pretty. They like them pretty girls what are smart.

I can't think no other way. My Dottie is gonna be fine. She's gonna fall in love and have lots of babies. And they're gonna look a lot like me. That's what I believe.

JB

1850

ALPHRETTA,GEORGIA

Them letters don't stand for nothin'. They was just the letter "J" and the letter "B." A passel of our mens was named TJ, BJ, AJ, and JJ. Don't know what it was about "J."

This is about me and one of Tote Williams' girls-the prettiest girl you ever laid eyes on.

Her name was Vagina.

That's right, Vagina Williams. Her mama heard the word somewhere and she liked the sound of it. Said it had a nice ring to it, like "Virginia" only better. The white folks called her "Vinny", but she was Vagina down in the quarters where it mattered. Anyway, that child was called Vagina for 'bout the first ten years of her life. Then Tote said that usn's should call his daughter Vinny. If a feller wanted a fight, he could let Tote hear him call Vinny by her old name.

Around thirteen, Vinny learned why her daddy had changed her name. At 'bout the same time all us learned what a vagina was. Inside a few days, the neighbor plantation knowed 'bout it. Then all the darkies for miles around knowed about the girl who's mama named her Vagina.

Vinny got all sad and down in the mouth. Then she reckoned she was famous.

The most famous colored girl that anybody had ever heard tell of. Vinny liked to hear the mens talk about her name and how pretty she was. Made the other girls mad.

Vinny began calling herself Vagina again.

Her poor old daddy git madder than a wet hen. Damn near lost his mind.

The first day I met Vagina, I didn't know who she was. She wouldn't tell me her name 'cause I'd get teased and run off. I just knowed she was built like one of them brick houses they talks 'bout and pretty as could be.

When I found out I'd been courtin' Vagina Williams, I was nail-spittin', stupid mad. I kicked the ground, and I kicked at the cat. But it was too late. I were in love.

The mens, the ones bigger than me, would say sumpin' like, "Hey, JB, I hear you done been sniffin' around Tote's old cabin."

Them fellers would fall all over each other back slappin' and laughin'. Then me and Vagina got married.

We jumped the broom down at the praise house and folks was real nice about it.

But the preacher giggled when he said, "Do you, JB, take Vagina...."

Vagina started laughin'. Everybody bent double over and bust up laughin'. The preacher was wipin' tears.

Preacher finally got to the part about "Do you, Vagina, take JB.... Peoples was dyin'.

We got through it, but there ain't never been a wedding like it. Marsa gave us a keg of corn whiskey. It weren't his good stuff, but it worked. We had a foot-stompin' good time that were talked 'bout for years.

I married the best-lookin' girl in these parts. And the most famous.

Tony R. Lindsay

ROSALYNN

1858

PHILADELPHIA, MISSISSIPPI

They weren't a better white man. Not around here. He was better than Jefferson, and that old Tom was President.

Jefferson done wrote, "All men are created equal." What he meant was all white men are created equal. And he didn't even mention women, never crossed his mind. That rascal weren't special, not in my book.

Now you take Marsa Sistrunk. There was a good man sho' nuf. He owned more than sixty darkies and not one of us was ever whipped. And, praise be to God, not one of us was ever sold. We had a nasty one in our bunch, and Marsa said he was gonna sell him certain. But we knowed he didn't mean it. Good to the bone, that was Marsa Sistrunk.

His Missus was good, too. She had a fellow make shoes for all the grown-ups. In the winter we had two blankets. And we had plenty to eat. Mind you it was not the fancy stuff that white folks ate, but it was good grub. White-people food would've turned our stomachs. Ain't nothing better than com pone if you got a little sumpin' to go with it.

Marsa did have a weakness. That's what his wife called it-a weakness. He liked us girls, especially the light girls. We didn't make a fuss about it. It was better than being bred to some fellow you didn't even know, some fellow who had never done nothing for you. Marsa wasn't pushy. He would let a girl know he was interested and it was comin'. He didn't give her a choice, but he weren't pushy. Not so as you could tell.

One thing that Marsa was sure on was that us girls have babies. Coloreds is valuable, you know.

Marsa Sistrunk was a Baptist and a good one. We was all Baptist. On Sundays we didn't hit a lick of work 'cept what had to be done. I mean the pigs had to be fed and the cows milked, but there weren't a hand in the fields.

At first we went to the white folk's church and sat in the back or outside, but some of them didn't like it. Anyway, we couldn't cut loose in the white church. Marsa, bless his soul, said we could build our own church. He said we could start by joining two cabins together and work on making it a real church. Soon, we had a praise house that we called the Full Gospel African Baptist Church. You should have seen it.

We didn't have a preacher, not one who could read. So anyone in the Spirit would get up and preach and talk about God.

We had old fiddle that was missin' a string. Willy was the best three-string fiddler you ever heard. You know what Marsa did? He gave us a brand new, in-the-box fiddle, never been used. We had home-made tambourines, drums and clap sticks. We sung the old songs. What a time we had.

We used the praise house for dances, weddings and funerals. Sometimes we would have a come-together for no reason at all.

Them was good days. But we knowed a dark day was comin'. Missus died first and next year God called Marsa to glory. Before he died, Marsa put in writing to say which of his chillin got which darkie. He tried to keep our families together. Marsa had three boys and two girls and they was good to us. Especially the girls was good to us. But it was never the same.

I say it was never the same after Marsa Sistrunk joined the throng around God's throne

Tony R. Lindsay

CLEOPATRA

1870

CLEBURNE COUNTY, ALABAMA

Marsa liked to give us fancy names. He named my cross-eyed brother Adonis. I never knowed why he thought it was funny. Down in the quarters, everybody called me Cleo and my brother Don. But when Marsa was 'round, we was called by them long names. I hated him for that.

The mens he called "bucks" and the womens "does." I'd rather be called a pickaninny than a doe. Anything but a doe. Gave us another reason to hate him.

Marsa drank plenty of liquor. When he was drunk he would want to see my nakedness, but he didn't touch me. Just wanted to see it. Said touchin' me would be like touchin' a frog.

One time when I had milk, he had me nurse his little boy for weeks. Marsa would not touch my skin, but he had his baby snuggle up to this frog.

After the war, when we was free, Cleopatra did not seem like such a bad name. So I kept it. Think it made Marsa mad. Hope it did.

There's a white buck in hell this very minute. The Devil must laugh every time he calls that bastard "Marsa." Like, "Hey, Marsa, is it warm enough in that corner for you?"

Ha!

Don didn't want no part of "Adonis."

Don's in heaven now, but he's still my little brother. I loved that boy. Always will.

SAM WESTMORELAND

1876

PASCAGOULA, MISSISSIPPI

My white folks wasn't rich. They had only one mule, a few acres, and two of us to work it-me and my twin brother. We was on loan from their kin.

Our Marsa was a good man and so was his boy. Young Marsa would work right 'long with us in the fields. He'd joke and cut up with us. Like the time I kilt a copperhead with my hoe. Young Marsa

51

said, "Let's tie that snake to Ronnie's hoe and put it under a plank so he'll have to reach under there to get it."

It was all the funnier 'cause Ronnie had a powerful dread of snakes. We tied the snake to the hoe and Ronnie put his hand right on it. He screamed, "Snake! I been bit by a snake. I'm gonna die sure. Tell Momma I love her."

Ronnie danced around pitiful. We was bustin' up. Young Marsa asked, "Is it painful, Ronnie?"

When Ronnie saw me and Young Marsa was all grins, he knowed he had done been fooled.

I threw my hoe down and took off runnin'. Ronnie picked up my hoe and come after me. He called his own brother a sumbitch. I swung 'round and headed back to Young Marsa. I stood behind him 'till Ronnie run up draggin' my hoe. At last, Ronnie made a little smile. Then we all laughed like we was plum silly.

When the war come, Young Marsa made ready to join up. His kin hugged him. Young Marsa told the snake story. Said it was the first time he knowed of that a colored boy had been bit by a dead snake. One of his kin said, "It don't happen that often."

We ate good grub and drunk good liquor. Me and Ronnie, too. Young Marsa promised to come home to help us get seed in the ground. He said if he didn't come home, we would know he was dead. His kin was wavin' and laughin' when Young Marsa rode off.

But nobody was laughin' when he didn't come home. They was cryin' then. We was all cryin'.

CHARLIE

1880

OGLETHORPE COUNTY, GEORGIA

Ol' Massa was a good one. I'll tell you that. There ain't never been a better white man that I ever heard tell of. Know what he did? He gave me a pass to go courtin' Maggie anytime I wanted to see that girl, which was 'bout every night. For sure my work had to be done afore I could ax to leave. But I always did my stuff and some extra. I was strong like a bull, don't you know.

"Charlie, you show this pass to any patrollers that stop you. And see that they give it back to you in case you run into another gang of 'em."

"Yes sir, I'll sure do that. I can't thank you enough for lettin' me go see Maggie. It means a whole lot to me."

"I can see that, Charlie."

Maggie lived about three miles from where I was born and raised. Didn't take me no time to cover them three miles. She would be sitting on the rope swing in front of her daddy's cabin down in the quarters. I'd walk up to her and flash a silly grin and just stand there for the longest time. Her daddy was always around somewhere, and he didn't allow no kissin'. He was a preacher and a man of God, don't you know.

The day came when I asked the preacher if I could marry Maggie iffin she would have me. I thought I'd choke tryin' to get the words out. We talked about Jesus for a long time, but he didn't give me no answer. When I was just about to die, he said, "You know Maggie is a Christian girl. You treat her right. You hear?"

I hugged that man 'til he hollered, "Put me down, Charlie!"

I sorta floated out of the door and over to where Maggie sat in

53

that swing. I was tryin' to find some words. Finally, I said, "I talked to your Pa."

"I know that," she said. "And I know what he said. I been talkin' to him myself. Now, Charlie, you got sumpin you want to ask me?"

God helped me to say it clear as a bell. "I want you to marry me. I want you to be my wife."

All Maggie said was, "When?" Then she stood up and we had our first kiss. Ain't never gonna forget it. Not until my dyin' day.

First thing the next morning I asked Marsa if I could marry Maggie. I got down on my knees and told him I knew Maggie belonged to Marsa Kindlewood, and she could not come to live with me, but I could go see her so long as he kept giving me passes.

"Get the hell up, Charlie. I've been talking to old Kindlewood, and he doesn't need Maggie as much as he needs a strong buck. I figure on trading my Joe for Maggie. What you got to say about that?'

I couldn't help cryin', and I couldn't stop cryin'. I tell you Massa was the next thing to Jesus. Maybe better than Jesus.

Before we was to jump the broom, Massa gave me the first suit of clothes I ever had in my life.

"This suit don't fit me anymore. Reckon it must have shrunk whilst hanging in the closet. It's kinda old and thread-bare but ain't anybody going to be looking at you. Not with what the Missus has got planned for Maggie."

What the Missus had in mind almost took Maggie's breath away. Missus bought a whole bolt of fine white cloth and had Maybelle make the best wedding dress any black girl ever wore in this part of Georgia, before or since.

54

The day we married my suit ripped when I tried to get into it. But Maggie's dress fit mighty proud. That silly Maybelle giggled, "Show it off, girl. Your daddy won't mind this one time."

I could not believe my eyes. Me, Charlie, about to marry the prettiest girl in the whole county, maybe the world.

These days, I ain't so strong. And sumpin is wrong in my belly. For nigh on to a month, I've been feelin' like the Lord is makin' ready for me. So, there's something I gotta say right now—Maggie's been a blessing to me every day of my life.

FARRIS LEE

1881

LOGAN, ALABAMA

Marsa Woster owned a lot of land, twenty grown plow-hands and a passel of women and chillin. We spent nights in log houses with dirt floors. The grown-ups ate pretty good 'cause they needed the strength to work. But the chillun didn't get much of nothing. There was a trough in the yard where the little ones got fed along with the dogs. Missus poured milk and mush and anything else she had in the trough, and we would scoop it up before the dogs got it all. Old Missus would laugh when them dogs growled and snapped.

We went to the preachin' at the white folk's church. We'd sit 'round outside while the preacher did his preachin' and peoples shouted. Then he'd come outside and preach to us. He told us the Bible said we gotta obey our Marsa and Missus. Preacher made sure we was all scared to death of Hell.

When the surrender come, Marsa said we was free. But if we'd stay with him, he would give us some of the cotton money and land for our own gardens. Most of us stayed on. The Missus didn't like giving coloreds land, but we knowed Marsa was a man of his word. Later, he said they weren't no cotton profit so he would give us extra land to make up for what we didn't get in cash money. I got twenty acres. He gave me papers and everything.

I walked all over them twenty acres. I touched the trees and stirred the dirt with my feet. Them were my trees. My dirt. Didn't belong to nobody but me. I spied a robin's nest in one of my trees. I thought to myself, "That's my nest. It's in my tree and it belongs to me." That's the way I felt. I thought, "That little stream there is my water."

Mr. Woster, that's what I called him after the surrender, gave me an old ax head, and I made a dandy handle. First thing I ever owned after getting' the land. I used the ax to cut down one of my my trees to make two round-bottom benches. They belonged to me. me.

I had plenty of wood to build a cabin. My cabin on my land. I wanted planks to put down a floor and never sleep 'nother night on the dirt. But I didn't have no saw. It takes a saw to make planks. Mr. Woster said I could borrow one of his saws, but old lady Woster threw a fit about it. Said I couldn't borrow nothin'.

I knowed a colored feller what had a saw, but he wouldn't let me use it lessen I give him an acre of my land. Told him I would give him a finger off my right hand before I would give him a bucketful of my land. Told him to go to hell, too.

LYLE HENDERSON

1882

ABERDEEN, MISSISSIPPI

I remembers when all our white folks was talkin' about the war. The War of Northern Aggression, they called it. They was sure the South would win and Jeff Davis would own the whole country, or maybe he would just give them Yankees a good lickin' and let 'em be.

Then we hears that the war wasn't goin' good. White folks said the Yankees was all dressed up real pretty and shootin' down their poor boys. Folks was sad about it. Then we hears that after the war is lost, all the coloreds is goin' be set free. I got real happy, but I didn't let the white folks know how I felt.

Marsa said if the South lost the war it would be bad for whites and blacks. He said blacks would likely starve when there was nobody to take care of 'em. I worried a sight about that. But then we hears that all coloreds goin' get forty acres and a mule from the gov'ment. I don't know how the story got started, but we all believed it.

Me and Jimmy went down to the barn to pick out our mules. We both picked the same one-Tatter. Jimmy said he saw Tatter first.

I said, "I called him first so that mule is mine when the war is over."

"Ain't your mule," Jimmy said. "We'll settle this right now. We'll fight about it. The winner gets his pick of mules."

Jimmy was older than me and a whole bunch bigger. I said, "It ain't right we should fight. Let's flip a coin." But we didn't have no coin. So Jimmy threw a horseshoe in the air and I called "Prongs up." I yelped when it landed prongs up.

Jimmy said the only honorable way to settle the argument was to fight. So I let him lay claim to Tatter.

The Yankees won the war and we was free. But I'm still waitin' for a mule. Never got no forty acres neither.

PREACHER POINDEXTER

1884

MURRELLS INLET, SOUTH CAROLINA

My white folks seen the war comin'. They said the South couldn't be beaten 'cause the Yankees didn't know nothin' about livin' in the woods and shootin' straight. Next thing I know, my ol' Marsa was ridin' off to the war on a fine horse. He looked mighty proud. Most of the coloreds wanted Abe Lincoln to win. Some wanted the South to win.

One day I spotted the Yankees comin' right up the lane towards the Big House. They wore little caps and carried fancy shootin' irons. They busted the door to the smokehouse and took all the meat. They set fire to the cotton gin. Then they burnt our plows. If they'd been half decent, they wouldn't burnt our plows and bent 'em up the way they did. They set the barns afire, but they left the house standin'.

Then one day ole Marsa come home leadin' a mule. Don't know what happened to his horse. He called all us together and said we was free. He asked us to stay with him 'cause most had nowhere to go, and he would pay us when he got money. Some left right away and never come back. Mammy said she weren't goin' nowhere, and I stayed with her. Ol' Marsa never did get enough money to pay me, but I stayed until Mammy died, about nine year. Then I hired out.

I joined the Little Creek Baptist Church, but they withdrew fellowship from me 'cause of my drinkin' and stealin'. After talkin' to the Lord all night, I got straightened out. The church took me back. When the old preacher died, I went to preachin'. I led the singin' and the shoutin'. They paid me for a while, and then they stopped payin' me. So I quit preachin'.

These days I drink a little, but I don't steal nothin'. I ain't gonna preach and shepherd no flock lessen they pays me. I'm talkin' about real money. I don't need no more chickens or sacks of flour.

BETTY LEE KILPATRICK

1891

BEAUTFORT, SOUTH CAROLINA

I belonged to Marsa R. L. Elsberry until I was fourteen-years-old. That's when the Surrender came and we was free. My mother and father was born on St. Helena Island. They took up together there on the island.

Marsa had almost a hundred of us. We lived in the Quarters. Two rows of cabins with a strip of land between the rows. All of 'em was one-room with a fireplace in the center and open on both sides.

Winter nights was my favorite time. We had 'bout fifteen folks sleepin' real close. Chillin mostly crowded around the fireplace. Grown-ups farther back. A kid could get powerful warm and snug when she had a fire in front of her and a sister or brother curled around her back. We was all in the same misery situation together. Most nights it was fun, but sometimes it weren't right to be doin' a lot of gigglin' when someone in the room was hurtin' bad after a whippin'.

The women got up before the sun to fix breakfast and somethin' to take to the fields for dinner. By sunup, a slave better have a hoe in his hand.

We worked all day and get back to the Quarters about dusk. Then worked in our own gardens till it was too dark to see.

Every year we had Happy Time. That was seven days at Christmas. That's when you got five yards of Negro cloth to make your clothes. You wore the same clothes all year. Our Sunday clothes was the same clothes we wore every other day. We didn't know nothing 'bout drawers.

We didn't work on Sundays, and we didn't have to go to

meetin' lessen we wanted to. Some Sundays, we got passes to visit family on other plantations. The patrollers made sure we was home before sundown.

The work was hard and the driver, sometimes a black feller, would give a lash to any slackers. If a slave did something really bad, he could be sent to the Work House in town. You die there. A slave in the Work House got a deep, blood-cutting whippin' once a week. Most prisoners died in three, maybe four, weeks.

When the War started goin' bad for the South and it looked like we was gonna be free, Marsa put Mommy and me on a boat to the mainland and then on a wagon. We bounced along till night. Slept under the wagon and started out again a day-break. Hadn't seen a soul when we got to his cousin's place 'bout dark. We stayed there more than two years.

One day the ol' cousin said her man was dead and the war was lost. We was free. She said we could stay with her or walk back to St. Helena Island.

Me and Mommy headed home. We got to St. Helena and found that the rest of the slaves had already been free for a whole year. Damn ol' cousin. Bitch.

The old house was burned up but the shacks were still there. That's where we lived until Mommy died. Then I moved to Beaufort. I'm free. But life ain't easy.

AVA MAE DAVENPORT

1898

BOLIVAR COUNTY, MISSISSIPPI

My old missus was a witch. She were mean to the bone. If she heard you talkin' something 'bout being free, she would wear you out with a leather strap. She weren't very big, and she weren't very strong, but that strap hurt awful bad.

She had to whip the slaves herself' cause her husband and two boys was killed early on durin' the war. I could've broke that little woman in half, but I had to stand there and take it.

The war news got better for darkies. We began getting sassy. So she hired us out. I went to Mr. Derreberry. One day he said to me, "Ava, there's been a surrender. Our boys are beaten, most of 'em dead. I don't have to pay your missus anymore. You are free."

I didn't understand what it all meant. I kept right on washin' and cookin' for Mr. Derreberry, but I didn't ask for no pay. It didn't seem right. I cooked meals for the family, and I always fixed enough for me. I ate the same good grub the white folks ate- pies, cakes, everything. I didn't have to eat no hoecakes or none of that trash. I ate on the back porch in good weather or sometimes in the kitchen.

There was a heap of trouble down at the courthouse. The Klu Kluxes wanted to kill a black boy for something they said he done. Them Kluxes rode up to the jail with white hoods on they heads and hoods on they horses down over they manes. I heard tell the sheriff said, "This here colored boy ain't done nothin' wrong. You ain't gonna kill him lessen you kills me first."

A Klux shot the sheriff down. Then four of them Kluxes got off they horses and shot the sheriff in the head all at the same time. Made a awful mess. They got the po' boy and cut him all over. They tied him up until them cuts mortified and he died.

The old sheriff's brother got himself elected the new sheriff. He made deputies of all his kinfolks, and they made out a list. Every now and again somebody what had they name on that list was shot in the head. Sheriff couldn't find out who done it.

The sheriff and his deputies put a bunch of Kluxes in jail for drunkenness and public vagraries. Sheriff commenced to say what a shame it would be if the jail accidently caught fire and burned to the ground. Awful shame, he said.

Them Kluxes knowed their time was about to come. They commenced to cryin' and prayin' and such.

Some big, important, office-holdin', white folks got wind of what the sheriff was sayin'. They got a message to him that if they was a fire at the jail, even if it was caused by lightning, ol' sheriff was gonna hang.

Well, the sheriff and eight deputies showed up in front of the jail. They was totin' rifles and torches. Peoples gathered up and down the street. There was the awfulest lot of wailing you ever heard comin' from the jail. Sheriff let them beg and carry on for the longest time. Then he let 'em go.

WILLY

1899

VESPER, GEORGIA

When I was a boy I had superstitions like my daddy. Took me years to unlearn some of the tales I was brought up with. I saw more ghosts than anybody I knows of. Most of them haints was my imagination, but one night I saw a sure-enough ghost. If you ever seen a real spirit, you'd know it ain't your mind playin' tricks on you. A man knows when he is lookin' at a real haint. A ghost don't say nothing. They mostly don't do nothing, but they want you to know they's there.

I was comin' by a graveyard and sippin' from a jar in a green cotton sack. Haints don't like green, ya know. The ghost looked sorta like a dog but was big as a mule and kinda blue and glowin'. I throwed my sack at the haint and took off runnin'. I was afraid to look back. I just kept runnin' and hollerin' for a half-mile 'til I got in Momma's cabin.

I couldn't tell her what I seen 'cause she would want to smell my breath and give me hell. I never been by another graveyard at night, and I ain't seen no more ghosts.

When the war come I was took to help the Southern boys. They had me look after the horses, but they wouldn't let me carry a gun. They said if I had a gun, one of them Alabama fellers might shoot me in the back.

Soon there weren't no horses or nothin' else to take care of. The Yankees done come through and took the animals and burn up everything there was to eat. Our men got so hungry they'd eat horseflesh if it hadn't been dead more than a day. They'd eat flat toads that had been squashed under foot, grasshoppers, anything. I got so skinny I couldn't make a shadder. A stray dog tried to bury me.

After we hears about the Surrender, soldiers set out walkin' in all directions. It took me most of a week to get back to the Wilkins' farm. Some places I walked through stink so bad of bodies layin' everywhere, I had to hold my nose. When I passed close to a feller, I'd look at they face. I'd think that's somebody's son, maybe somebody's husband and somebody's daddy. Wonder where they home was and what they life was like before the war.

Marsa Wilkins' house was most burnt down. I said, "Marsa, I've come back to you if you'll have me."

He said, "Willy, I'm not your master anymore. You don't belong to anybody. You are free. I need lots of help if you will work for food. I don't have any money."

We shook hands and I stayed on for fourteen years till he died.

He left me this patch of land where I still live. When I moves from this place, it will be to Glory.

OLIN WASHINGTON

1900

OPELIKA, ALABAMA

I's a proud man. Nobody never give me nothin' after I was free. They should've let us homestead. The country had plenty land that didn't belong to nobody. And trees enough to build houses with plank floors. We could've cleared land and planted gardens. But they turned us loose like a bunch of cows.

I hired out buildin' chimneys and cuttin' wood for white

folks. Didn't spend a dime except to get sumpin to eat. I scraped enough money together to buy this little plot. Thirty acres bought with my money.

If I could've got a better start, maybe I be richer today than a lot of white folks. I say maybe because Ku Kluxes might have come after me. Guess the Lord knows best.

Ellen-that's my wife-told me that the Lord helps them what helps themselves. She studied 'bout it a lot. Ellen said folks get rich by having their own business. "We got to make somethin' and then we got to sell it."

I said, "All we got is thirty acres, one mule, one cow and her calf, and 'bout three dozen chickens. We ain't got nothing to sell."

"We got chickens. We'll sell eggs."

She was right. We always had plenty of chickens and eggs and soon we had plenty more. I commenced to tryin' to sell eggs along the road leadin' to town. But peoples already had eggs. And they weren't gonna pay me for sumpin they already had. I got down in the mouth. I said, "What we gonna do with all them chickens and eggs?"

Ellen studied on it some more. Then she said, "Ain't no place in town for colored folks to eat. Right?"

"Well, they can eat outside on them benches behind Barney's and a couple of other places."

"Yeah, but no place where they can sit down at a table and eat like they's home. We'll get a little place in town. You know peoples love my chicken sandwiches and wild- root tea. We could serve collards and beans from the garden. White folks won't come near it, but we'll have all the colored trade. And there's a sight of colored people in town most days."

"It won't work. We have the chickens, plenty of root, and the best spring water around. But we ain't got no money to start a diner."
"Talk to Mr. Miller. He owns some of those empty houses on the end of Main Street. They's all run down but one of them places

would be fine for what I got in mind."

I said, "You fry up the bestest chicken of anybody in these parts. But it won't work. The chicken will spoil by the time we get it to town."

"We'll keep live chickens in cages behind the diner. Talk 'bout fresh chicken!"

I met up with Mr. Miller. I told him 'bout my idea. I told him that considerin' he was the biggest man in town in more ways than one, he wouldn't be scared to rent to a colored feller.

"I ain't scared of nobody, Olin, you know that."

"Yes, sir, but 'bout the rent. I ain't got hardly no money. I thought maybe I could do some work for you so as to pay my rent by workin' real hard. I can do most anything."

"Those houses aren't making any money just sitting there. You pick one and set up your business. If you make a go of it, we'll talk about rent."

"I can't thank you 'nuff, Mr. Miller."

When Ellen heard what Mr. Miller said, she when to jumpin' and clappin' her hands. I got a week's worth of huggin' and kissin'.

We was proud of that diner. We called it "Ellen's Chicken and Tea."

BILLY RAY LEE

1902

KNOX COUNTY, TENNESSEE

I ain't never believed in ghosts, haints, conjures, and such like. Some of them saltwater colored what come by boat brought their superstitions with 'em from they homeland or them south islands. They would sit around a fire pit at night and tell us chillin 'bout voodoo spirits that done snatched up boys and girls what would never be seed again lessen they came back as spirits theyselves. Some shore-born Negros believed they stories, but I never did. Still, it could make a feller feel uneasy like.

I disremember most of them stories they told us, but Saltwater Sally was a woman not to be took light. I recollects we was sittin' by the fire when Sally told a chillin' tale.

Once Sally started in, Mama said I could sit real close to her, but I was too big to sit on her lap.

Sally told about a haint what carried his cut-off head under his arm. He weren't a bad sort until one night he sat his head down on a big rock. The head rolled off the rock and down a hill.

The haint couldn't see to find his head. His head could see, but had no way to move about.

I got as close to Mama as I could get. Then I seed Sally was lookin' straight at me. Thought I might die. Sally hollered, "Billy Ray, you got the right side of yo' face in your mama's bosom, but turn yo' head to the left and see what is sittin' right beside you."

No way! I weren't gonna turn my head to see some slimy devil with his head on his lap. Weren't gonna happen. A mule couldn't have pulled my head away from Mama.

One time, Marsa gave me a note to take to his cousin, Marsa

71

James, a bunch of miles away. It took me to dinnertime to get there. Then I had to wait till suppertime while Marsa James finished some business and wrote a note for me to take back to my Marsa. On the way home the sky got darker and the woods got spooky. The wind picked up and the shadders was gettin' long and movin' about in the wind. I got scared. Then a blackbird flew low right over my head. That bird was tryin' to tell me to turn back. I know that now.

Then I seed the possum. Dead he were -deader'n hell-but alive too. It was like he were dyin' though, what with them glassy eyes. Glassy they were except for tiny slits in the centers. Dreadful little beast he were. Couldn't stomach the sight of him. Made my skin wiggle like it was tryin' to get away. I got a powerful dread down in my soul.

I say he were mostly dead. He smelled dead. It was a bad odor. It were like the worst kind of manure you can imagine. No, it was worse than that. Older, with a core stink that could peal paint off a barn door. I seed a crow fall right out of the sky. That stink could kill a grown mule.

It were his hind parts that died. He dragged himself along using his front legs. Nubs they were. Pitiful I tell you. But mean too. There was some deep down mean in that possum.

I kept goin' deeper into the woods. Then I heard it. Sumpin' was comin' along the trail behind me. Then a thought hit me like a bolt of lightnin'. It were that no-head haint!

Right then, I got religion. God told me not to believe in ghosts and nonesuch. He told me to walk, don't run, He said for me to keep singin' out loud over and over, "They ain't no ghosts, they ain't no ghosts." Promised God I would walk sorta casual like and not run a step.

I begun, "They ain't no ghosts, they ain't no ghosts, they ain't…." Then I heard it fo' sho'.

That haint begun to sing, "They ain't no ghosts, they ain't no ghosts" The sumbitch must have done found his head, and now he was mockin' me. Whoo-ee, I was gonna be one of them voodoo spirits sho'nuf. Then I reckoned what I was hearin' were an echo.

I sung, "They ain't no ghosts, they ain't no ghosts."

Right away I heard, "They ain't no ghosts, they ain't no ghosts." It was a dang echo.

I sung real happy like, "They ain't no ghosts in these old woods."

It came back, "They ain't no ghosts." Oh, Lawd, it weren't no echo-it was that voodoo haint.

Right then, I broke my promise to God. I run like I never run before. I swung around trees and leaped over briars and thickets. My hands and feet was bleedin' awful, leavin' a trail for that haint.

Didn't matter. Marsa's finest hoss could not have caught up to me. I would have left a bobcat pantin'.

I made it home, body and soul in one piece.

It never happened again. I mean, I never had another run-in with a ghost. Today, I don't believe in voodoo, spirits, or none of that stuff.

But, in case I'm wrong, I don't go into the woods if I can help it. I'm always home before dark. And I don't go near a graveyard.

Descendants of Lucas Lee

WESLEY LEE

1940

BULLS GAP, TENNESSEE

My father was a tall, strong, stem, no-nonsense kind of man. Fiercely religious, Dad considered himself to be a soldier in God's army, a prayer warrior opposed to dancing, drinking, and movies. I loved my father, and I feared him as well.

At the age of nine, I visited with the family of my friend Otis Lee Harper. The atmosphere in his home was warm and relaxed. Mr. Harper wore an old sweatshirt and Mrs. Harper had her hair in rollers.

It was time for dinner and time for Otis Lee to say the blessing. His face lit up with a mischievous grin. He blurted, "Lord, bless the meat, let's eat."

Otis Lee was beaming with his clever remark. His parents laughed and hooted. Mrs. Harper asked where she had gone wrong to raise such a naughty boy. Old Grandmother Harper looked toward heaven. "Lord, Otis Lee ain't right. You know he ain't ever been right."

The following evening it was dinnertime at my house.

My family waited for me to say the blessing. As always, Dad donned a tie and Mom had on her makeup. I began with some traditional words, and then I suffered a dreadful brain lapse. My mouth spewed, "Lord, bless the meat, let's eat."

Holy cow! What was I thinking? Was I tired of living? When did I decide to tum my tender behind over to the mercies of an angry saint?

Dad's face turned darker. Then the darkness drained away. I lost feeling in the lower portion of my body—a condition I hoped would last through what was about to happen next.

Then the numbness was replaced by an urgent (and somewhat tardy) need for bladder control.

Sweat poured down my face as Dad's lips began to move. "Boy, if you ever do anything like that again, I will…"

He did not finish the sentence, but I knew that servant of God would heap righteous wrath upon my skinny body. Goodbye, backside. It would be toast.

The keyword in my father's statement was "again." It meant he would spare my life for the moment. But, he could change his mind in a heartbeat.

Not another word was spoken during dinner. Even Mom did not break the agonizing silence.

Our home was unusually tense for the next twenty-four hours. I felt like a condemned prisoner waiting for a call from the governor. At exactly 6 PM, we sat down for the evening meal. It was not my turn to say the blessing, but I knew what to expect. My father whispered in a voice loaded with a terrifying promise. "Wesley will say the blessing tonight."

I tried to speak, but all I could do was wheeze. I started over. Finally, I began by thanking the Lord for hard-working farmers who toiled in the fields to grow broccoli and turnips, and for truck drivers who brought vegetables to market. I thanked God for the loving hands that had cooked a delicious meal. I mentioned something about sailors in peril upon unruly seas. Then I asked for permanent fair weather the world over. I prayed for my mother, and her mother, and mothers everywhere.

I asked for a quick recovery for the sick and afflicted, including a special blessing for anyone suffering from diphtheria or diarrhea. I pleaded for the kind treatment of the world's animals, especially puppies. I expressed concern for people who committed, "Sins of the

only were they scraping in poverty, they were under the fist of a tyrant.

Dad asked where we should put the food and clothing. "In the kitchen," responded a chorus of eager voices.

Dad approached the door leading to the kitchen. A rough two-by-four was nailed across the doorway at about knee height. The plank served no purpose and appeared singularly out of place. Dad was puzzled. "What's this?"

The kids glanced to their mother for a reply. "Jack put it there. It's his way of being nasty."

Flabbergasted, Dad asked, "Do you mean everyone has to climb over this doggone board every time they go in or out of the kitchen?"

Aunt Mayella lowered her head.

Mom was outraged. "How long has it been there?"

"Long time," came from a moppet in the crowd.

Dad snarled, "I'm going to kick that stupid plank down right now."

There was a collective gasp as the children sucked in as much air as their lungs would hold. Aunt Mayella pleaded with Dad. "Jack will be mad. I'll catch an awful beating for sure. Oh, please don't touch that board."

Dad relented, all the while chewing on his lower lip the way he did when he was really angry. I wanted to become a man as strong as Superman and beat Jack Doggins within an inch of his life. Then I climbed over the obstacle and followed Dad into the kitchen.

Another distressing memory involved my pretty little cousin, Mary. At age six, she was bright, energetic and outgoing despite the deplorable conditions in which she lived. Mary had a wide smile and perfect profile. Without her one defect, Mary would have been a lovely girl and sure to become an attractive woman.

The problem involved her right eye which did not coordinate with the left. The right eye always peered inward toward the bridge of her nose. When she looked left and right, up and down, only the left eye moved.

A group of physicians in Forsyth County donated their services on a rotating basis to indigent patients. A member of the four-doctor firm performed one operation free of charge every month. A lady at the local church knew about Mary and put her name on a long waiting list. When Mary's name finally reached the top, the church lady persuaded Uncle Jack to allow a physician to examine Mary.

The doctor reported that surgery to correct the problem would be simple. He would clip a tiny ligament that held Mary's eyeball in a fixed position. The remaining eye muscles would compensate for the severed tissue, and Mary's eyes would eventually coordinate perfectly. However, the procedure had to be performed soon while Mary was still growing and her muscles developing. All that was needed was Uncle Jack's signature giving consent.

Jack Doggins flatly refused.

He absolutely would not listen to anyone about the matter. Nothing could be done. The mere mention of the topic could bring terrible retribution on Mary.

It was the only time in my life that I ever heard my straitlaced, devoutly religious dad call anyone a son-of-a-bitch.

Mom said, "Honest to God, I think I could watch him hang."

I last saw my cousin when she was seventeen years old. She still had the quick smile and bubbly personality. With her eye tucked into a comer, Mary was not a beauty. But Mary Doggins was a beautiful person.

TYRONE LEE

1954

FORSYTH COUNTY, NORTH CAROLINA

"But, Mom, the poor devil is dead. Are you sure it's right to be cheering?"

"Son, you should understand that the poor devil was a snake and a disgrace. He's dead, thank God, and he's not coming back."

With unbridled exuberance, Mom had learned the news of the death of her brother-in-law, Jack Doggins. To reinforce her contention that Jack was a worthless scoundrel, she reminded me of the story of Uncle Jack's son, Morgan, the eldest of twelve children.

My cousin was an introverted, hard-working boy determined to make the best of life despite being raised in poverty. When Morgan was thirteen, he incurred the wrath of his drunken father regarding a missing hammer. Uncle Jack could not find the implement and accused his son of losing it. He and Morgan were rummaging in a shed when Uncle Jack finally found the tool beside a rabbit coop right where he had left it. He picked it up and strode over to Morgan, who was searching through another corner of the shack. Without warning, Uncle Jack brought the hammer down hard on Morgan's left kneecap. Uncle Jack stomped out of the building, leaving my cousin screaming in agony. Morgan walked without ever bending that knee again.

With his slight build, stiff leg and no education, Morgan had little choice of occupation other than physical labor. When he was eighteen, Morgan found work in a cement factory in Tennessee. One afternoon he was working on the rim of a concrete mixer that churned out twenty-ton batches. Extending his left leg straight behind him, Morgan reached down to pick up a nozzle beside his right foot. A co-worker said that he had watched in horror as Morgan lost his balance and fell into the giant machine. Eight feet long bars stirred for several seconds before the shocked witness hit the emergency stop button. There was little left of Morgan Doggins.

Uncle Jack was unmoved by the gruesome death of his son. "Damn fool, should have been more careful."

When Jack was drinking, he would administer what he called a "general purpose whipping" to the first kid he could get his hands on. Even his mentally handicapped daughter wore the bruising and scarring.

Uncle Jack died shortly before his forty-fifth birthday.

As soon as Mom heard the news, she screamed with delight and telephoned her sister, Mayella, Jack's wife. My aunt was elated. "He's dead as a stump. I saw him two hours ago, stiff as a preacher's prong."

"Calm down, Sis. What are you going to do about some decent clothes for the funeral?"

"Mount Harmony Baptist Church is taking care of everything. They're giving us clothes for the kids, but I could use a dress for myself."

Mom promised to provide a new black dress.

On the day of the funeral, my large extended family showed up, along with a surprising number of curious folks.

All funerals in those days were accompanied by a lengthy sermon. It was customary to extol the virtues of the dearly departed while admonishing the sinners among us to mend our ways.

The Reverend Willard Guthry had graciously agreed to provide solace to the family. "Reverend" was a title that Guthry had conferred upon himself. Before his conversion to religion, Guthry had been known as a carouser. But the Lord had spoken to him as he made his way home after a night of consuming illegal spirits, and Willard Guthry renounced sin and dedicated his life to God's work.

He became sort of an assistant to the pastor of Mount Harmony. The funeral of Jack Doggins was a God-sent opportunity for Reverend Guthry to demonstrate his oratorical talents.

When Mom, Dad and I entered the church, we were seated in the section reserved for the family behind Uncle Jack's widow and their eleven surviving offspring. The Doggins kids were a happy, boisterous group now that their life-long persecutor lay cold and lifeless. They had evidently tussled over a mound of second-hand clothes on a first- come-first-serve basis. Their outfits selected for color and flash, with little regard to size and fit. Some of the girls wore frilly dresses that dragged on the floor, while other girls proudly displayed frocks so short as to be indecent in the pious environment of Mount Harmony. My male cousins selected shirts, ties, pants, suit coats and sport coats without concern for coordination. A few boys wore coats with sleeves ending two inches above the wrists. Other boys had only their fingertips visible.

Reverend Guthry ascended the four steps leading to the pulpit in a dignified and stately manner. He cleared his throat as a signal for the kids to shut down the clamor and pay attention to the proceedings. A buxom soprano sang, "When We All Get to Heaven." After she struck the final note, she took a seat in a most demure manner beside Reverend Guthry.

The kids sneaked glances at one another to determine if applause would be in order. One of my cousins said, "What the hell, let's give her a hand," whereupon the whole group began enthusiastically clapping. A couple of the boys emitted shrill whistles. The preacher, taken aback by the breach of church etiquette, glared at the Doggins clan and the applause trailed off.

With the sermon about to begin, several kids chose to reshuffle their positions on the hard benches. One of the older girls took extra care in arranging herself comfortably while contending with a skirt designed for a much younger female. The process did not fail to capture the attention of Reverend Homer Guthry. He appeared mesmerized for several seconds before straightening his tie and returning his attention to the lectern.

The sermon was less than profound. However, a moment of high drama occurred when Reverend Guthry announced he had good news. "By the grace of God, your own Willard Guthry, humble servant of the Most High, has been chosen to tell you people something that will warm the cockles of your hearts."

Parishioners looked up and the kids stopped fidgeting. The preacher swelled with pride as he proclaimed, "Brother Jack made his peace with the Lord! Yes, you heard it right. You heard it here. Brother Jack Doggins will wait for us in Heaven forty paces inside the eastern gate."

A collective gasp erupted from the congregation. Aunt Mayella fainted straight away. Two ladies rushed to her aid brandishing paper fans. Cousin Jeff shouted to his siblings, "It ain't true! That dipstick, sumbitch preacher made up that story, sure as shit." Uncle Jack's daughters moaned and wailed.

Reverend Guthry was about to go further with his good news when Cousin Jeff stood and demanded, "Tell us what the hell you mean. Say you made it up."

Jeff showed no intention of sitting down until he got an answer. Rumbling swept through the audience.

Guthry, clearly shaken by the outburst, called for calm and explained that he had visited Jack Doggins on the day of his passing. "Brother Jack eagerly accepted the offer of salvation just minutes before he went home to be with God. His sins were instantly forgiven. Brother Jack is surely standing this very moment in Heaven."

Jack's oldest daughter, Reba, got on her feet, turned to the congregation and shrieked, "He ain't in Heaven! He's right there, dead as a flat possum."

All order and decorum broke down. Rumbling became pandemonium.

Aunt Mayella regained consciousness. She must have known it was time for action. She stood and told Jeff and Reba to sit down.

Tony R. Lindsay

The preacher was about to speak when Aunt Mayella ordered him to have a seat and listen to what she had to say. Reverend Guthry, to his credit, did not utter another word.

"Kids, listen to your mother. This little preacher don't know beans about your daddy. But we know how he hurt us, and we know he ain't in Glory. Jack would say anything to save his skin, even lie like a dog to a wet-behind-the-ears preacher. God is good. No way will Jack Doggins ever get near the doorstep of Heaven. He can't hurt us anymore. We can all go to the Blessed Kingdom someday without fear of ever seeing that devil again."

Cheering and applause burst from the Doggins children and quickly spread throughout the congregation. Mom shouted, "Glory be to God!"

The kids began hugging anyone within reach. Aunt Mayella was engulfed in the embraces and kisses of her children. Mom led a spontaneous chorus of "Give Me That Old Time Religion."

Untangling herself from the mass of bodies, Aunt Mayella straightened her pretty new dress and made her way up the aisle, acknowledging the ovation of friends and family as she passed. We stood respectfully as eleven children followed their beloved mother out of the church and into the bright sunshine.

JOHN THOMAS LEE

1955

BURLINGTON, NORTH CAROLINA

We showered and sat down to a dinner of "cathead" biscuits, country ham, and real milk, not the wimpy store-bought kind, but milk that two hours earlier had been sloshing around in ol' Blossom. Only the calf got fresher milk.

Cathead biscuits were about the size of a man's fist, served piping hot and loaded with gleaming churned butter. Rivulets of hot homemade maple syrup flowed down the groves in the mound of bread and swept butter into swirls. Each biscuit had enough calories to sustain an ordinary person for a day or a farm boy for about three hours.

I was spending two weeks with my cousin in the Burlington community about fifty miles from my home in Winston-Salem. Bill and I had worked hard all day in sweltering heat cutting and stacking tobacco for flue curing. He was two years older, almost eighteen.

Bill fixed a wicked grin on me. "Hey, city boy, you got the guts to go with me to the Blue Rooster? I've been there before. Blacks have to sit at the bar. No tables for Negros."

I knew for damn sure that I didn't belong in a tavern catering to hard-drinking white men, but I was not about to chicken out. We drove to the honky-tonk in my uncle's black 1940 Ford coupe and pulled onto a gravel parking lot lined with battered cars and trucks.

"Come on, punk. You're about to have an experience you never had in Winston-Salem."

Bill pushed open the heavy, creaking door. I almost choked. Smoke from a dozen cigarettes and several cigars created a dense haze and the smell of a wet dog. Patsy Cline's "Crazy" blared from the jukebox.

Two walls were plastered with Chevrolet logos. The Ford boys gathered under their blue oval. Massey Ferguson had more posters than John Deere. Pabst Beer had equal billing with Miller High Life.

I heard snippets of Bill's conversation. "Sorry about your heifer, Frank. How's your alfalfa doing? Did that big bull decide he likes the ladies?"

"Oh, hell, yeah. He loves the ladies. And I don't turn my back on him."

I tried to look older and tougher than I felt.

"Who's the kid?" a guy with a gaping grin asked.

"Aw, that's just my cousin. He ain't nobody. He's a city boy from Winston- Salem."

Bill motioned for me to follow him to the bar, where he squatted on a stool and yelled, "Hey, Randy. Gimme a beer."

"Beer, my ass," I muttered. Bill was underage and a good Baptist boy. He couldn't be serious about drinking beer.

Randy hiked up his jeans over his ample belly and looked to me for a drink order. "I'll have a Pepsi, please."

Fatso smirked as he pushed the soft drink in front of me. I glanced around to get the lay of the place, being careful not to make eye contact with anyone. Several rode-hard women, a few tattooed with vulgar phrases, crowded around a pool table. A couple of bleached blondes shared a spittoon with their brawny male companions.

Patsy Cline settled into "Back in Baby's Arms."

A beefy guy invaded the space beside me. "How's it going, negra?"

Call it intuition, but I got the impression this was not going to be a pleasant encounter.

"I'm fine."

"They tell me you're a sissy from the city. 'Zat right?"

"I live in Winston-Salem."

"No shit!"

He hooted and pounded the bar. With my eyes, I pleaded with Bill to get involved in the conversation.

"Aw, Lonnis, why don't you leave him alone? He ain't nuttin' no how."

Lonnis shut down the laughter like turning off a faucet.

"Tell you what, Bill. I'm gonna kick this city boy's black ass."

"Why you wanna do that?"

"'Cause, you little prick, I'm gonna beat the crap outta him."

"Aw, Lonnis, you already scared the crap outta him." There was a tiny bit of truth in my cousin's statement.

Bill was not going to be much help. He was shorter than me and even scrawnier than my 150 pounds. Gorilla-man towered over me and weighed around 260 pounds. Lonnis kicked my shin with his heavy boot and gave me a hard poke in the ribs. He was just warming up and getting nastier by the minute. It was time to do something, even if it was wrong.

I snuck a look toward the door. Maybe I could get out of the joint before anyone could stop me. Lonnis caught me eyeing the exit and rotated his barstool to face me. I said goodbye to my best option.

The maniacal gleam on Lonnis' face spurred me to formulate a new plan. But I needed courage. I picked up Bill's longneck Budweiser and took the first swig of beer to ever pass my lips. "Ugh, pour this stuff back in the horse."

Perhaps it was the beer, but from somewhere I felt the impulse to go for it and hope for the best. Bracing my feet firmly on the footrest of the bar, I turned my shoulders and torso to the right as far as possible. Surging adrenaline shook my body. I wheeled around, driving my fist into Lonnis' face. I heard a pop as the middle knuckle of my right hand cracked on the point of his chin. I ran like a madman for the door.

Once outside, I felt the exhilaration of the night air as I raced for the darkest corner of the parking lot. I hurtled into thick undergrowth and scrambled up an embankment onto a dirt road.

My feet flew along the ground. If Lonnis and his friends could run twenty mph, I could run thirty. If they could run thirty, I could do thirty-five. And run all night if I had to.

About 200 yards along the track, I stopped and listened for the sound of anyone coming behind me.

Silence.

I had to get my bearings and think about what to do next. A dirt road leading to my cousin's house intersected the highway about a mile from the tavern. Leaving the path and keeping close to the four-lane, I made my way through the dark woods. Branches and briars ripped my arms and face. Blood oozed down my neck.

After what seemed like hours of scrambling through the brush, I saw on the other side of the highway the road to Uncle Claude's farm. I scanned left and right for headlights. Any vehicle could be loaded with Lonnis and his friends. My actions might have upped the ante of the conflict to the point where my life was on the line.

A couple of cars zipped past, and then no headlights were visible in either direction. I hauled ass across the highway and into bushes on the other side. I felt my way along the dim road, constantly checking ahead and behind me for headlights. Then I heard a dreadful sound—the crunch of tires on gravel thirty yards behind me. My heart fluttered. I couldn't feel my legs below my knees. The grinding racket came nearer, and I heard voices as I stumbled off the road and dropped on my back into a shallow ditch. An old pickup rumbled louder. The truck veered side to side as the driver searched for the road in the darkness. I held my breath.

"Watch where the hell you're goin'."

"Shut up. Gimme a beer."

The truck skidded to a stop a few inches alongside my head. "Get your own damn beer. We're gonna kill that negra."

"We ain't unless you shut up. He ain't deaf, you know."

The engine revved and tires inched forward. Pebbles spewed by a front tire landed on my chest. Eternity lapsed before I heard the rear wheels beside me.

"Anybody got a rope. We'll hang the sumbitch just like they used to."

"Got to find him first."

"Hanging's too good for his kind."

"Gimme that friggin' beer."

The noise and the voices faded and feeling returned to my toes. I had been lying in two inches of mucky water. I got on my feet. I stopped to listen after each step, then after every three steps, and finally every thirty seconds.

At around midnight, I topped a hill and saw a lone, dim light on the front porch of my uncle's farmhouse. I crept closer, making sure an old truck loaded with thugs was not parked in the gloom. When I was certain no country hooligan was hiding in the scrubs near the porch, I dashed for the door. It was unlocked.

Within minutes, I climbed onto a couch beside Bill's bed. He stirred. "Where the hell have you been?"

"Forget about me. What about Lonnis?"

"The peckerhead was out cold. You broke his jaw. Anyway, I didn't hang around there, me being black, and you being my stupid cousin. That bunch will sober up and come lookin' for you."

I had to think of a way to get my young ass out of Burlington and back in the city where I belonged.

Flue-cured tobacco!

My ticket out of rural hell. First thing the next morning, I placed a call to my father. "Hi, Dad. Hope you're okay, but you got to come and get me right away. I'm dying for sure."

"What seems to be the matter, son?"

"I've got the Tobacco Flu. It's the worst kind of influenza. It'll kill a fellow in a heartbeat if he doesn't get miles away from raw tobacco. Guess I'm a goner. Tell Momma I love her."

"Son, there's not the ring of truth in what you're saying. But I'll pick you up at noon. I have an idea you'll feel better when we get you back in the city."

Dad and I drove past the Blue Rooster on the way out of Burlington. I took a long look at the place where I almost died of fright, and where I discovered I had more courage than I thought.

MACK LEE

1959

HARRISBURG, PENNSYLVANIA

We pulled to the curb in front of a weathered house in Old Salem. A robust lady greeted us with a wide smile and hearty handshakes all around. She led us to a detached garage. A mother dog-a mixed breed terrier-sprawled in an industrial-sized "Ajax" carton stuffed with two tattered blankets. Four puppies crawled over her.

Dad counted noses. "I understood you had five puppies?"

"Yep, there's another rascal around here somewhere."

Right on cue, a little mutt poked his head out from behind a red Radio Flyer. He waddled toward me with his plow-point skimming the floor.

"That's him. He's into everything."

Mom and Dad cackled at the new arrival. The white pup had a black spot resembling a saddle on his back. A black ear and black eye on the right side gave him a comical, offbeat appearance. Picking him up, I offered no resistance to about a dozen warm, wet licks. Imagine finding the best dog in the world only a mile from my house.

The lady provided a cardboard box filled with layers of newspapers, and we were on our way home with my new playmate and best friend.

Mom said, "You will have to take care of him."

"I will, I promise."

"We're going to need a name for him."

Tony R. Lindsay

Dad sniggered. "Let's call him Stripe. It's a funny name for a dog with spots."

"No way, Dad. We're going to call him Ajax."

"Ajax it is, son."

We arrived home and Dad carved a section out of the box so Ajax could get in and out. The pup regarded the container as his toilet. We provided another box, complete with a red doggie dish and water bowl. Mom folded her arms and tapped her foot on the floor. "You have two days to build a doghouse, and then I want that dog out of my kitchen."

As weeks went by, Ajax never grew tired of my petting, and I loved every sloppy lick. The number one dog on earth seemed to think I was the best kid in the world.

"He's a smart dog, Dad."

"Why don't you teach him a few tricks?"

I tried to instruct Ajax to roll over, sit, and fetch. He was smart all right, but he had no interest in higher education. He spent his days investigating every inch of his surroundings and sniffing everything that didn't hop or crawl away.

At the age of five months, Ajax discovered our neighbor's big gray cat creeping across our yard. Ajax cautiously approached the tabby's rear. The cat rocketed into the air and sprinted away at full tilt. Ajax seemed emboldened by the experience. He pranced up to me. I could almost hear him say, "Did you see that?"

Another episode of chasing that cat convinced Ajax that he was a cat-killer. One morning I saw the tabby slinking along near of a pile of lumber in our woodshed. I picked up Ajax and made sure he caught sight of his prey. Without a bark, Ajax sped away and rapidly closed on the defenseless creature. But, this time, the startled cat did not bolt for cover. The cat bowed his back in a menacing arch. Every hair stood on end. Saber-like claws were unsheathed. White dagger teeth glistened.

Ajax's eyes almost popped out of his head. He tried desperately to put on the brakes and change course all in the same motion. Tumbling over the ground, he came ever nearer to a house cat that had morphed into a mountain lion overnight.

He finally came to a stop on his back. He seemed to realize with horror that his most sensitive parts were within range of the claws of Dracula Cat. His eyes reflected the prospect of agonizing dismemberment. Each leg jerked independently in a spasm of every-leg-for-himself!

At last, Ajax got his legs organized and underneath him. The cat hissed malicious intent. Death-dealing forelegs fanned the air. Ajax seemed to shrink and shudder before launching an all-out, hell-for-leather retreat.

He accelerated as never before. Listening to the dreadful howling, one would have thought the poor dog had already lost a limb to the heartless predator. He shot past trailing a foul odor.

Ajax must have thought the bloodthirsty critter was only an inch from his tail. His stubby legs blurred as he found a gear that would tax a Greyhound.

Seven seconds and about ninety yards passed before Ajax risked a glance over his shoulder. The god-awful-cat-monster was nowhere to be seen. Another hundred yards, and Ajax bravely whirled to face his enemy. He barked a fierce warning in the direction of the woodshed.

From that day forward, Ajax regarded any cat as a panther that hadn't eaten in a week. When he spotted a cat, he immediately established a separation of about fifty yards. Then, his forelegs pawed the ground as if preparing for a charge, but his back half made ready for an instant, breakneck retreat. Barking with absolute contempt, he would look up at me with his head cocked to one side.

I could almost hear him say, "Did you see that? It's a fuckin' cat!"

Ajax and I were best friends for the next three years. Nothing could separate us. Nothing, that is, except his intense devotion to romance.

One day I watched as my canine Casanova approached a mixed-breed. She was much larger than he, but Ajax seemed to be blissfully unaware of the disparity. They circled each other a few times. With introductions completed, Ajax was ready to make his move. A rawboned hound appeared on the scene. He looked mean. I expected to see my pampered little terrier make a quick exit the same way his courage had vanished in the face of a cornered cat.

This time, it was a different story.

Ajax snarled viciously. He lunged, snapping his jaws on the animal's throat. A bloody, horrific struggle sent up a cloud of dust. Ajax was ready for a fight to the finish. He finally released his grip. His opponent was exhausted. The wounded dog slunk away, and Ajax completed his mission without interruption.

Two more similar incidents occurred within a month. Ajax displayed ferociousness totally alien to the friendly little pooch that I loved. Far more powerful dogs chose not to take on a fierce little terrier willing to die for his cause. Taking a bone away from a Mastiff would be easier. Chasing trucks would be safer.

He would disappear, sometimes for several days, in quest of romantic encounters. When he showed up again, he was often bleeding and battered. He would lie around, eating little, and drinking copious amounts of water. Within twenty-fours, he would regain his appetite and his health.

Each time a receptive female came within range of his super-sensitive nose, he would be off again.

Dad said, "Son, someday Ajax will encounter a much larger and just-as-mean dog. And that will be the end of your little companion."

Ajax had been gone two days when he shuffled into our yard.

94

His black ear had been chewed to a nub. Blood caked a dozen lacerations. The routine of resting and drinking began as usual. The The morning after his return, I approached him with a bowl of his favorite canned dog food. He did not move. His eyes were glassy, his breathing shallow. All day Ajax clung to life. I prayed for his recovery and prepared for the worst.

At last, the little warrior struggled to his feet and looked up at me. I could almost hear him say, "I'm feeling better, and I'm starving."

My friend lived many more years, but he never again sought the affection of females. His days as a lover and a fighter were over.

LIONEL LEE

1961

KNOXVILLE, TENNESSEE

Grandpa Luke Lee sneaked a sly grin. Then he explained why he had ten children. "When it rains in the country, it's too wet to plow."

"Not exactly a romantic notion, Grandpa. If Grandma heard you say that, you'd be in big trouble."

"That's why you're not going to tell her. And if you do, I'll deny it."

My efforts to document something of my Dad's family were rewarded when I uncovered a juicy family secret—but more about that later.

My father, William Ralph Lee, was born in 1912 in Campbell County, Tennessee, the fifth child of parents who descended from slaves. Seven boys and three girls kept my grandparents hopping. Grandpa owned and operated a trading post and grocery store. His customers were about evenly split between black and white. One afternoon, he was behind the counter weighing lima beans when a Cleve Elders came into the store.

"Luke, I been a good customer for a long time. Ain't that right?"

"Yeah, it seems like a long time to me."

"And I've always paid my tab. You know it's true."

"Well, you've been late a lot of times, and you never pay up completely. In fact, I want to talk to you about your balance."

"Before you start, I got to tell you something. Times are hard, and I ain't hardly got no money. I ain't ever gonna be able to pay you nothing on my tab."

Grandpa winced, but said not a word.

"You're a good church-going man, Luke. I know you ain't mad."

Cleve turned and started for the door. On his way out, he spied a side of bacon hanging on an iron hook.

"That's some mighty fine bacon. How much are you getting for it?"

"Nineteen cents a pound."

"That's a fair price. I'll take a couple of pounds."

Grandpa wanted to throw the deadbeat out, but a sale was a sale, and he sliced two pounds off the sixty-pound hunk of meat. After wrapping the bacon, Grandpa held the package in his left hand and extended his right hand with the palm up. "That will be thirty-eight cents."

Cleve fumbled in his pockets. Then he looked Grandpa straight in the eyes. "Say, Luke, I ain't got no money with me. Do you mind if we start a new tab?"

"Wh-h-att You got the balls of a giant, and I'm going to blow them off your ass right now." Grandpa lunged for his double-barreled shotgun. He tumbled a stack of canned goods onto the floor. He got his hands on the weapon and whirled around as the front door slammed with a loud bang. Grandpa said, "I can laugh about it now, but I was plenty riled that day."

Dad told me that his father was a strict disciplinarian. "Talking back" to Grandpa was unthinkable. I asked Dad what would happen if a boy complained about a chore.

"Let's say he told you to gather eggs. You could grumble if you wanted, but you better be grumbling on your way to the henhouse.

With twelve mouths to feed, and a store and a farm to run, Poppa didn't tell a kid to do something a second time."

Dad's oldest brother, Claude, functioned as Second Dad. He had authority to give direction to his nine younger siblings. With Grandpa spending six long days a week at the store, it fell to Claude to operate the modest farm. Chickens, hogs, and cows had to be fed. A large garden provided vegetables for the family or for sale in the store.

The family's old farmhouse had been constructed as a two-bedroom home. The back porch was closed in as a third bedroom. Grandpa, Grandma, and the baby boy had one room, and the three girls had another room. Six boys were crammed into the tiny porch bedroom. The situation was complicated by the fact that Claude did not share a bed with any of his brothers—an acknowledgement of his high rank as Second Dad. Five boys were allocated two narrow platforms: two boys warmed one mattress, and three boys slept crossways on a padded shelf.

Dad remembered flexing his knees to prevent his feet from hanging over the side.

Years later when Claude moved out of the home, Dad was promoted to a mattress that he shared with only one brother. Dad recalled climbing into bed the first night and stretching his long legs to their full extent, luxuriating in the expanse of sleeping lengthwise. He found it difficult to go to sleep. Before dozing off, he pulled his legs up into their accustomed position.

In the foothills of the Great Smoky Mountains, temperatures would often fall below zero. The drafty old farmhouse was heated only by a wood-burning stove in the main room. A cooking stove in the kitchen provided some warmth during meal time. Each night everyone went to bed at the same time, climbing into their long johns with button-up trap doors. Guys and girls gathered around the main stove and warmed their front sides then turned their backsides to the heat.

Toasty warm, they dashed off to bed.

On really cold nights, blankets were replaced by a two-inch thick comforter. Dad said it was like sleeping between two mattresses. Comforters for the girls were stuffed with goose feathers, which were in short supply. The boys slept under comforters filled with chicken feathers. There was no shortage of chicken feathers on the farm.

I asked Dad how the horses, cows, and pigs fared during the freezing winter nights. He said farm animals handle cold temperatures differently from people and pets. As long as they have shelter and are out of the wind, animals can easily survive the coldest nights. I wondered what a horse would say about how easy it was to stand all night in an unheated barn at five degrees below zero.

Saturday night was bath night. Two large galvanized tubs were taken to the kitchen from their storage pegs on the side of the corncrib. Water was heated to fill one tub. Grandpa and Grandma bathed first. The tub was cleaned and fresh water heated for three girls. When they were finished, the tub was cleaned, and this time water was heated for both tubs. Tub number one was allotted to three boys. The four youngest boys were assigned to tub number two. A week of grime turned the water to the color of coffee. Clean sheets were brought in from four clotheslines that stretched from the corncrib to a storage shed. The whole clan slept well on Saturday nights.

Sunday morning, Claude drove to church in the smaller of two wagons with his mother and sisters on board. They were followed by a larger wagon with the remaining family members. Grandpa held the reins to two strong, unruly horses.

Dad loved the sight of carts, wagons, and folks on foot arriving at Indian Creek Baptist Church near Lafollette. About twenty families attended most Sundays. The church was spiritual center and social hub of the community. Men talked about the weather and the progress of their crops. Women talked about everything else. Children ran and played in the churchyard before and after services. Pre-teen boys and girls whispered, "Who do you like?" or "I know who likes you." Teenagers were usually seen in pairs. A couple was considered to be courting if they sat together in church for two consecutive Sundays.

One of my uncles told me about the time when he and four of his brothers tried to scare my father half to death. Dad was thirteen, and had gone courting for the very first time. He had finally gotten the courage to walk Lulu Cardwell to her home after a revival meeting. Her house was about a mile from the church in the opposite direction from the Dad's home. His brothers schemed to be waiting along the spooky road on Dad's return trip. Dad suspected something might be up, so he took a shortcut through a vacant field that was as dark as ink on the moonless night. Dad knew the location of every tree and boulder in that meadow, and he reasoned that there would be no brothers with whom to contend. About halfway through the three-acre parcel, Dad heard movement directly ahead of him. Surely, one of his stupid brothers must be crouched in the dark. Dad charged ahead with a yell intended to scare the wits out of a country boy.

Instead, he slammed into a creature far larger than any brother. The monster must have weighed more than a ton. And it was warm and hairy. Dad recoiled with a terrified shriek.

His brothers, hiding along the road, heard the yelp. One boy shouted "Ralph forgot about the cows!" Then Dad remembered that several cows had been moved earlier that day from the north pasture to the field that he had chosen for a shortcut.

My uncle said, "There was big ol' Ralph standing in that field yelling like a wet baby. I laughed so hard that I fell on the ground. He must have been thinking about that little Cardwell girl. Scared the poor cow half to death. The next night I mentioned to Ralph that I was going down to the church. I asked if he would come along in case I needed protection. I thought he was going to kill me."

"Uncle, there have been a lot of jokesters in our family, beginning with Grandpa, and you inherited his sense of humor."

"Well, if the flu shi...I mean if the shoe fi...How does that go?"

Another uncle told me about a family secret on the condition that I never mention it to Dad (he need not worry). A girl in her late teens with long straight hair struck up a friendship at church with one of Dad's sisters. My aunt was three years younger and the alliance seemed a bit unusual, but my aunt was pleased to include the attractive teenager among her friends. Eventually, the girl said she would like to sleep over. Arrangements were made for an overnight visit.

On a warm night in June, after the family and their guest had been in bed for about an hour, the girl slipped out of her place beside my aunt. She tiptoed into the room where six boys were supposed to be asleep. She stretched out on the floor beside a bed. She reached up and touched an arm. Dad's brother was already wide awake.

The girl displayed an inviting posture. My uncle sprang onto the floor and quickly took advantage of his good fortune. Perhaps he was too quick. The girl was not ready to call it a night. She looked up at another boy with his eyes about to pop out of his head.

Dad's brother told me, "Here was this beautiful girl, night gown around her waist, on her hands and knees, back arched, looking back over her shoulder, and smiling as if it were the most natural thing in the world."

A second uncle (or was it Dad?) rolled out of bed and descended into heaven. The other boys looked on in disbelief. Two sated boys received lingering French kisses before the girl made her way back into bed beside my aunt. Thus, both boys experienced sex before they ever enjoyed their first deep kiss.

"You know, boy, the kissing usually comes first."

"Yes, I know."

My uncle said the family and their guest sat down to breakfast the following morning. The meal was accompanied by a lot of silly grins, sidewise glancing, and an inordinate amount of giggling. After breakfast, the entire family waved a fond farewell. Grandma announced without explanation, "That girl will never set foot in this house again."

In the days before sewer systems, all families had outhouses. The Lee family had two. One for the boys, located east of the house, one for the girls on the south side. The eight male members had a "two-holer." Females were provided with a more demure single-hole facility.

Store-bought toilet paper was a luxury, but one the family insisted upon. Sears and Roebuck catalogs and dried corncobs were useful backup.

Clean water was not taken for granted in rural areas in the 1920's and 30's. Gutters channeled rainwater from the roof of the house into a pit called a cistern. Another cistern near the barn provided water for the farm animals. When rain was insufficient, water was hauled in buckets from a spring about ninety yards from the home. Girls never hauled water. That was man's work. More exactly, it was boy's work. Every boy participated in the chore and three sizes of buckets were available for the task. The smallest boys toted the smallest buckets. When a boy became strong enough to handle a larger bucket, he enjoyed a rite of passage.

The spring served another purpose. Water oozing from under rocks at the bottom of the spring was almost ice-cold on the hottest summer day. A watermelon or cantaloupe left floating in the pool for an hour made a delicious treat. The melons were cracked open on a large rock and the center consumed on the spot. The kids did not have to be frugal when eating a watermelon. Melons were plentiful, and provided a rare opportunity to eat only the choicest part of something and discard the remainder.

In 1929, Grandpa bought a used Model T Ford. The entire family was proud of their new acquisition. No one was more enthusiastic than Grandpa. He enjoyed listening to the engine. In fact, he loved everything about the car, but he flatly refused to learn to drive. The driving was left to Claude.

Several years later the family acquired a large touring car, a second-hand Buick with an open top and luxury seating. By that time, Claude shared the driving with the next three oldest boys, including my father, Ralph.

Dad told me about the time when he drove seven members of the family in the Buick to visit a relative. The road to his aunt's place had been built on the least-resistance principle. The route had been minimally cleared and wound around trees and other obstacles-fine for a horse, but difficult for an automobile. The road road tilted left and right with the undulating terrain.

Dad approached a left turn at approximately ten mph. The left side of the Buick lifted off the ground and, for a moment, seemed poised to drop back on its tires. Then it rolled onto its right side. Everyone spilled out of the vehicle and began tumbling down the slope.

Grandpa got to his feet and ran around to see if anyone was seriously injured. After determining that no one was hurt badly, Grandpa focused his attention on the driver.

Dad said he expected to get the tongue-lashing of his life, maybe worse.

"Ralph, you did a great job. It could have rolled on top of us. Come on boys, I think we can get her back on her wheels. Let's have a go at it."

Grandpa and the boys were able to right the car and push it around the treacherous curve. Everyone piled back into the Buick and resumed their journey.

The Great Depression hit the family hard. Grandpa's customers had little money. Neighbors to whom he had extended credit for years could not pay their debts. The store had never earned much income, but then it ceased to make any profit. The Tennessee Valley Authority provided some relief when they offered to buy the farm and store. The land would be at the bottom of a lake when a dam was eventually constructed on the Tennessee River.

Grandpa closed the store, sold his property to the TVA, and moved the family fifty miles to Knoxville. Grandpa worked wherever he could find a day's work. Dad said he and his brothers labored at any task that provided even the smallest income. Food was basic and scarce, but the family was never really hungry.

***

My mother, Polly Ethel Randles Lee, grew up hungry. She was born into a family of twelve siblings. The Randles lived near the tiny village of Kodiak, Tennessee. There was nothing "Walton-like" about Mom's upbringing. Her mother died when Mom was nine years old. Mom's dad left much of the care of his family to the two oldest children. Meals often consisted of potatoes-nothing but potatoes.

Grandpa Randles spent much of his time in pursuit of backwoods widows. One day he brought home a woman and her five children to meet the Randles gang. The families were sitting on the front porch and in the yard when the widow's young son crawled over and sat down in the middle of a planter and began pulling up the flowers one by one. No one did anything to stop him. Momma, at age eleven, lifted the little boy out of the flowers and gently set him on the grass. Then she handed him the flowers he had already pulled up. "Here, honey, you can shred these."

The widow's oldest boy was about eighteen. He stalked over to Momma. "Don't touch that child," he shouted. Then he slapped Momma so hard that she landed on her back. She lay there, writhing in pain. The boy smirked and looked defiantly at Grandpa. He was much stronger than the old man and he knew it. Grandpa marched into the house and returned with his shotgun. "You apologize to Ethel, or I'm going blast you into eternity." The boy hesitated and Grandpa pulled the hammer back on his weapon.

The boy's mother screamed, "Apologize for God's sake. Do it now!"

Finally, the bully said, "I'm sorry. I apologize."

That incident is the only story I can recall where Grandpa Randles showed real gumption. To be fair with Grandpa, he was an orphan and abandoned on the doorstep of the town doctor and his wife. They resented having the boy in their lives, and they were cruel to him. As a pre- teen he supplemented his meager diet by catching turtles and boiling them in their own shells. Who can say they would have turned out any better under the circumstances?

Mom taught herself to read and write and, at the age of twelve, she left home with no formal schooling. An older sister, the beloved Mamie, was living in Knoxville and made room for Mom in her cramped apartment. The sisters remained devoted to one another throughout their lives.

Mom and Dad met in Knoxville. He was a friend of a friend, lanky, broad-shouldered, but not especially handsome. Mom said of her attraction to Dad, "I knew in my heart that he was a good and kind man."

Then I asked Dad what his thoughts were when he first met Mom. "That's easy. I thought, oh, my Lord, what a figure. It doesn't get any better."

Mom shrieked, "Ralph Lee, you hush. You should be nice."

Mom was easily embarrassed by any reference to her bountiful silhouette. Dad would say something while grinning like a schoolboy on his first date. Mom's face would plush and she would admonish him to be nice. Dad would raise his arms to ward off fake blows. Whatever Dad had said passed over my head, but Mom seemed to have no doubt that he deserved a pounding.

"Let's get him, Mom. We'll teach him to be nice."

How they must have enjoyed my naiveté.

***

My parents married in 1936 and moved into a one-room apartment above Carroll's Store on Western Avenue in Knoxville. Mom became pregnant in 1938, but her health was not good. She was unable to work. Then, Dad lost his job.

The winter of 1938 was bleak for the couple. Mr. Carroll consented to collect no rent until Dad could find a permanent job. With the coming of Christmas, Mom and Dad agreed there would be no gifts exchanged between them that year.

On Christmas morning Mom was standing at the stove preparing

105

breakfast when Dad sauntered into the kitchen with a sly, apologetic expression on his face. He held something behind his back.

"Ralph Lee, what have you done? I told you not to get me anything."

"Well, I didn't get you much." Dad brought forward a white box of Dewey's Chocolate Covered Cherries.

"Oh Ralph, you shouldn't have. I love you very much."

They stood there in the kitchen, hugging. Mom was sobbing and tears rolled down my father's cheeks. He said, "Don't worry, baby. We're going to be just fine."

As tough as times were, they got worse in early 1939 when Mom gave birth to an unhealthy child. She suffered greatly during the delivery. My parents named their son Donald Ray, but he lived only about thirty-six hours. In those days, the infant's condition was known as "Blue Baby." Deficient flow of oxygen caused by a malfunctioning heart valve gave the skin a blue shade. After Donald Ray died, Mom was confined to bed for a week. She said those were the saddest days of her life.

Mom's doctor told her that she would never be able to have another child because of damage done to her by the arduous birth of Donald Ray. Mom and Dad would never need to practice any sort of birth control.

In 1940 Dad had a steady job but the wages were low. Mom worked for a man known as Breezy Wynn. Herman D. Wynn was a self-made millionaire and former football hero at the University of Tennessee.

During the autumn of 1941, Mom did not feel well. She agreed to see a doctor. After her examination, Mom waited for the physician to re-enter the room. He came in with a long face and seemed to be pondering a difficult diagnosis. Then he broke into a wide grin. "Mrs. Lee, I have news for you. You're pregnant!"

Mom went home with the good news for Dad. They held each other close. Mom said, "Ralph, let's pray right now."

They got on their knees and with hands folded they leaned forward onto the cushions of their sofa. Together they asked God to allow the life within Mom to become a healthy child.

On the morning of December 7, 1941, the Japanese struck Pearl Harbor. Mom gasped when the news blared from the radio. She realized Dad would likely join the Army. He would probably be on a battlefield somewhere when the baby was due in July of 1942. He might never come home. He might never see their baby.

Mom said she quickly got control of her emotions that day. Nothing could be allowed to endanger the chances for successful delivery of their second child.

The war economy began to boom. Dad got a good job at the Aluminum Company of America. Because the job involved the production of materials for the war, Dad received an occupational deferment. He never served in the military, although three of his brothers fought in Europe and two in the Pacific.

On July 2, 1942, Mom gave birth to a healthy baby boy. That would be me. I grew up as an only child, much loved by parents whom I loved dearly.

JACK LEE

1962

DETROIT, MICHIGAN

South Central was the domain of ruffians, crooks, and ladies who were generous with their affections for a price. Officer Gus Koon walked the South Central beat along with his formidable partner in law enforcement, the renowned Tarzan Gwinn.

Tarzan towered six feet eight inches and weighed more than 350 pounds. Monstrous arms extended at an angle from his sides to accommodate bulging biceps. His eyes were set deep under a prominent brow ridge.

On the morning of my sixth birthday, Logan Koon, son of the policeman, and I were playing cops and robbers in his back yard. He was always the cop pummeling the bad guy with fake blows. Logan would take a swing, missing my chin by a few inches, and I'd flip over backward as if hit by a wrecking ball. But that day my friend lacked his usual enthusiasm. He slunk inside to talk with his mom. I watched the door close behind them and then cast around for something else to do.

Officer Koon and Tarzan Gwinn were repairing a car in the Koon's detached garage. I ambled inside the wide door to see what they were up to. The big men were laughing about a woman in bed with a guy named Arthur Ridas. It made no sense to me.

Mrs. Koon appeared in the doorway with her son in tow. "Logan has not felt well all morning. I'm going to heat up some chicken soup for him."

"What's wrong with you, boy?" Tarzan asked in his brisk manner.

"Nothing."
"You look mighty peaked to me."

"Ain't nothing wrong with me."

"Gus, I better have a look at that boy of yours."

"Go right ahead."

"Get over here, kid."

Logan shuffled forward and stood directly in front of the giant policeman. Tarzan knelt on one knee and looked Logan up and down. Then he inspected behind each ear. "Uh huh, ah yes, uh huh. Stick out your tongue, kid. Uh huh, it's just as I thought. This boy's got ancestors!"

Blood drained from Logan's face. He wobbled before regaining his balance. "I ain't got 'cestors. You can ask anybody. Momma, tell him it ain't so."

The veins in Tarzan's neck bulged. His face glowed. "Yep, you got ancestors, boy, sure as anything."

I took a step back. Ancestors could be contagious. I figured it was some god- awful disease worse than the trots or whooping cough.

"There's something else, boy. I hear that you slumber on your pillow every night."

"It ain't true."

"That's not what I hear. I heard that you even slumber in the car."

"It's a lie. I don't slumber on nothing. Dad, you tell him I don't slumber."

Tarzan Gwinn was enjoying the joke immensely, but Logan was on the verge of tears. Mrs. Koon gave Tarzan a look that would scare a ghost. She took Logan by the hand and led him out of the garage. "Come with me, son. We're going to have a little chat."

Tarzan Gwinn howled with laughter. "Did you see the look on his face?" For my part, I was not sure if Logan had ancestors or something milder. I skedaddled home to tell my mother about my desperately ailing friend.

About six years after the "ancestors" episode, I was talking with Officer Koon in his front yard. A police cruiser, tilting to the left as if it had a broken spring, slowed to a stop along the curb. The driver's side door opened wide and out rolled the massive Tarzan Gwinn.

"How you doing, Gus?"

"Afternoon, Tarzan."

"Where's Logan?"

"He's around here somewhere."

"Good. I got to talk to him. I need to tell that boy a few things about girls. I got some good stuff to lay on him."

Our attention was snapped away by the loud bang of a screen door. Mrs. Koon marched onto the porch. She had her hands on her hips and a narrow-eyed threat on her face. "No, you don't, Tarzan Gwinn. You are not going to tell Logan anything about girls. I don't want my boy spending the rest of his life in therapy."

MOSES LEE

1964

SPRING VALLEY, ILLINOIS

Momma wanted me to become a preacher. She said I could have my own television show and get a hundred-dollar haircut and wear better suits than a Mafia don. But I always wanted to be the first black Catholic in Spring Valley. Catholics on television drink a lot and wear some neat stuff. Our small village had only one Catholic family. They gave me the name and telephone number of a church in a town thirty miles away. I called them up.

"Hello. Is this Saint Luke?"

"Not really. This is the office of Saint Luke's Parish."

"I want to talk to the head honcho. I want to be a Catholic, and I got some questions for him."

"One moment, please."

I had to hold the phone for almost two minutes. I decided some Catholics could be a little slow on the uptake. Then a man's voice said, "How may I be of service?"

"I want to be a Catholic and a good one too. I'm almost thirteen and I don't know a bunch about it. I want to be Pope or one of them Cardinal fellers. But I'm okay with starting as a priest. I figured we should talk."

"Indeed, I believe we should talk. Can you come by my office? I'm Father Frederick."

"I'll be there. My uncle has already said he'll bring me to meet with you guys."

"Fine. I'll see you in the morning at ten. By the way, what is your name, young man?"

"Everybody calls me Moses."

"See you tomorrow, Moses."

Uncle Charlie dropped me off right on schedule. "You must be Moses."

"Yep. And you must be Father Frederick. Can I call you 'Pops?' "

"I prefer 'Father Frederick.'"

The priest was a nice guy and a baseball fan. We talked about a lot of stuff, and I got around to telling him about my plan to do as much research as possible about my idea that beautiful girls have a beautiful nakedness and that plain girls have a plain nakedness.

I told him that with all those nuns around I ought to have plenty of opportunity for research.

"Son, there is something you should know. Priests are celibate. Always have been."

"You don't say. I'm a Democrat myself."

"I'll try to explain. First of all, I know dozens of nuns and none, or maybe one, who would be interested in your research. Anyway, celibate means that you do not have sex."

"Oh damn! I mean darn. Are you telling me that a priest has no sex? Are you telling me that Pete and the boys will have to go?"

"Relax. No operation is necessary. But as a priest you cannot have sexual relations."

"I never did think sex with relations was a good idea."

"You still don't understand. What I'm saying is that you can't fool around with girls."

"Not ever?"

"Never."

"Oh, Lord. I don't want to tell Pete about this. He's gonna sulk. I can tell you that."

"Moses, I think you should forget about being a Catholic. Maybe you could be something lesser, like a Presbyterian. You could be a minister."

"Do ministers have sex?"

"Not so much. Maybe you could be a Baptist. You could become a deacon or a preacher."

"Do them guys have sex?"

"Lots of it from what I hear."

"Then it's set. I'll be a Baptist preacher just like Momma always wanted. I'll give them sinners hell, you can bet on that."

"Go in peace, my son."

"See ya later, Father."

I shook Father Frederick's hand and headed for the door. "Oh, Moses."

"Yes, Father?"

"Lay off the Catholics. And let me know how it goes with your research."

"We'll stay in touch."

"Moses, one last thing."

113

What's that?"

"You don't have to give me the details about, you know, your research-unless you want to."

CARL LEE

1967

VALDOSTA, GEORGIA

"George is an incredible guy."

"You got that right. Nothing he says is credible. You've got a lot to learn about George," my friend responded.

"George told me that he served in the Medical Corps of the Marines, performed emergency surgery on the battlefield, and took the lives of about three dozen well-armed enemies. He suffered as a prisoner of war for a year. Him being black and tall, he stood out among the prisoners and they gave him extra torture. Then he was associated in some capacity with the Space Administration."

"All bunk. George has an active imagination. He reads something, and after a while he's convinced he's had the experiences he read about."

"But what about all those medical terms he throws around? He knows something about medicine."

"Like I said, you've got a lot to learn about George."

George Everett, the maintenance man at Magnum Extrusions, knew the workings of every apparatus. He had little formal education, but was a brilliant guy. He read everything from Popular Mechanics to Paleontology World.

George walked with a pronounced limp. I asked him about it. The hitch was the result of a war wound. An explosion had blown off the lower leg of a soldier. George had charged into the field, applied a tourniquet above the knee and carried the man to safety.

When George went back for the severed limb, he sustained severe shrapnel wounds but managed to retrieve the soldier's leg and pack it in ice. With George's assistance, a physician reattached the appendage. The brave infantryman became a marathon runner but George never completely recovered from his injuries.

George said, "Man, that's ironic, ain't it?"

I mentioned the heroic battlefield episode to my co-worker. He said, "I've known George since we were in grammar school. He's never been in the military. He's hobbled all his life. George tried to get in the Marines, but they wouldn't take him because of his bad leg. Let me tell you something..."

"I know what you're going to say. I've got a lot to learn about George."

George drove a worn-out old Buick. He assured me that the Roadmaster was an exceptional automobile. When I expressed some skepticism, he informed me that he had personally made a circuit around a superspeedway at 146.403 miles per hour. "I was doin' about 180 down the backstretch."

George confided in a low voice that the famed race driver, Lee Petty, had modified the Buick's engine. "Lee built it for me. He made me promise that I wouldn't tell anybody my Buick ain't stock."

I swore not to reveal to a living soul the secret to the outstanding performance of that sedan.

George Everett was not the only exceptional employee of our small company. Sharon Belews was our receptionist, mid-twenties, black, almost skinny, and voluptuous. Tight curls framed inviting eyes and pouting lips. Sharon wore expensive outfits that accentuated her natural charms. Truck drivers invented reasons to go to the office with paperwork so they could get a look at Sharon. She enjoyed a little flirtation and gave the guys something to talk about with their buddies.

One of Sharon's most ardent admirers was a profoundly handicapped man we employed to do repetitive tasks. Paul came to work each morning and did his job for about forty-five minutes. Then he would shuffle over to a window to wait for Sharon's car to pull into the lot. His face was stuck to the window like Garfield's. Paul's vigil was rewarded when Sharon rather casually got out of her car and retrieved her purse from the back seat. Sharon could have placed her purse on the passenger seat, but she had a generous nature. The purse was always on the back seat necessitating a memorable contortion.

Sharon would sashay across the parking lot and disappear around a comer. After a long sigh, Paul would return to his duties.

Sharon was often the topic of ribald conversation among the men in the factory. On a day when she wore a black and white outfit designed to give men heart palpitations, George and I were standing near two mechanics as they joked and laughed.

"Did you see her this morning?"

"Did I see her? I almost fell off my forklift. When she maneuvered up those stairs, I could hear symphony music. She ain't nothing but a sailor's dream."

George held back his assessment of Sharon. The maintenance man had a dignified demeanor befitting a man of his accomplishments. When we were a few yards away from the other men, George said, "There's something I want to say about Sharon."

"What's that?"

"She reminds me a lot of my wife."

"What? You're kidding me."

"If my Naomi was Sharon's age, they could be identical twins. I didn't want to say anything about my wife in the presence of those men. You know how guys are."

Did George's wife ever look as good as Sharon? I had to find out. I asked his old friend from grammar school about George's wife. "Why do you ask?"

LATISH LEE JOHNSON

1968

WILMINGTON, NORTH CAROLINA

I entered my home through the side door and heard Aunt Wilma talking in hushed tones with the lady who lived next door. I listened for a few moments from the breakfast room.

"Your niece will be valedictorian of the senior class next year, that's a lock."

"I'm so proud of her. One more year of high school, and she's never had a single 'B'. Nobody can top her. There're only a few black kids in her class, and our Latisha will be valedictorian." Then Aunt Wilma's terrible words pierced my soul. "Bless her heart, she's smart, but she's not pretty."

"What a shame. She's a sweet girl, caring, unselfish, and so intelligent. Too bad she's not attractive."

I turned away and hurried to my room. Then I stood in front of a full-length mirror. It was true. I wasn't pretty. My high-bridged nose didn't seem to belong to my face, but the real problem was the 230 pounds spread over my 5'5" frame. I loathed my puffy cheeks and the sagging pouch under my chin. I sat on my bed, picked up a pillow and held it to muffle the sounds of sobbing. I would have given anything, even the dream of becoming valedictorian, to be attractive and sexy.

The school year at Wilmington High was winding down, and I had never had a date. No guy had indicated the slightest interest in me, and I was terrified by the prospect of never having a boyfriend, never experiencing sex and never having a family of my own.

I would have loved to discuss my fears with my classmate, Jennifer Owens. Jennifer seemed interested in me as a person, but I suspected plumpish Jennifer enjoyed being around a girl who made

119

her appear petite by comparison. She said, "I'll tell you a secret, Latisha. The gang will spend a lot of time at the pool this and I'm going to buy a yellow bikini and keep that dowdy green handy in case Mom and Dad show up at the pool."

I hated the thought of the kids having fun, laughing, and flirting, while I sat at home on my fat ass.

My parents were on an Alaskan cruise to celebrate their 25th anniversary, and I was lonely. I wanted to get far away from Wilmington.

Uncle Jason and his wife invited me to spend the summer with them in Knoxville, Tennessee. I would be able to relax and have plenty of time for my passion for reading. I eagerly accepted their invitation.

The eight-hour journey began by driving west on I-40. The old four-door Chevrolet was in good condition despite its dull appearance. I thought, *"Nobody will ever think this crate is a Ferrari, and nobody will ever mistake me for a fashion model."*

A mile west of Winston-Salem, I prepared to exit the interstate near a McDonalds when a late-model SUV loomed in my rear-view mirror. The damn driver had his head turned toward the passenger seat. Oh, my god! I tried to pull off the exit ramp. But there was no time.

The impact sent my car straight into a guardrail. The old Chevy had no airbags, and my face was smashed on the steering wheel. I can't remember anything else.

I awoke to the glare of bright lights. I could not speak and everything hurt, even my hair. A voice said, "Dear, you have been in an accident. Your nose is crushed, and your jaw is fractured in two places. Now, you must sleep."

Sometime later I was in a recovery room. My jaw was wired closed with only enough space to pass a straw between my lips.

Uncle Jason was standing by my bed. "Honey, you're in

Wake Forest Baptist Hospital. You're going to be okay. When you are out of here, you can come to Knoxville and recuperate at our place."

Two days later, the doctors said I could leave the hospital the following morning. My face was healing, and the broken bones could be reconstructed at The University of Tennessee Medical Center in Knoxville.

I arrived at Uncle Jason's home and moved my stuff into their guest room. That night I weighed myself for the first time since the accident. Unbelievable!

The trauma of the accident and several days of having nothing but liquids had dipped my weight to 208 pounds—the first time I had weighed less than 210 in more than two years. I set a goal of weighing less than 200 pounds within three weeks.

The next day I met with doctors at UT Medical Center. "Miss Johnson, what kind of a nose would you like?"

The doctor explained that the bones in my nose had been splintered and complete reconstruction would be necessary. I could have my nose shaped to my liking by a team of physicians performing plastic surgery. I smiled as best I could.

I had always hated the shape of my nose, a gift from my father and from his white father before him. This was my chance to have a slightly dipping line from the top of my nose to the tip.

When the bandages came off, I spent a lot of time turning my head from side to side. I tried to look past the swelling, bruising, and wired jaw. I noticed something. My face was thinner than before.

I asked Mom and Dad to allow me to remain in Knoxville and that they should not to come to see me until I was ready to see them. I wanted this more than anything and they agreed.

I was released from UT Medical Center and eagerly weighed myself on the bathroom scales at Uncle Jason's—the same scales that last indicated 208 pounds. I held my breath.

The dial stopped to the left of the 200-pound mark. If I could have opened my mouth, I would have shrieked—196 pounds.

I established a new goal of 180 pounds, and I exercised as much as a liquid diet would sustain.

Six weeks later my jaw was unwired. I tipped the scales at a disappointing 182. But I was more determined than ever to lose weight. My senior year would begin in just four weeks.

I jogged every day. I had not eaten solid food for so long that I had no difficulty adhering to a diet of 2,000 calories per day.

My parents settled out of court with the driver of the SUV. He had been reaching for another beer from a cooler. The award was $250,000 plus medical expenses.

I had a new look and more money than I ever dreamed possible. However, I still weighed around 170 pounds when it was time to return to school to begin my senior year.

My friends in Wilmington knew about the accident, but the only people back home aware of my facial surgery were Mom and Dad. I didn't want to see my family and classmates until I reached my ultimate goal of 140 pounds.

My parents told school officials that I was not fully recovered in the fall. They obtained permission for me to take correspondence courses for two months and promised that I would be in school as soon as classes began after the Christmas break.

I continued rigorous exercise and careful dieting. But, I had one more step in mind. I wanted sex appeal. I wanted cleavage.

When I re-entered UT Medical Center for breast augmentation, I weighed 163 pounds.

Aunt Linda suggested one final, less dramatic, procedure. I had never given much thought to my hair. But Aunt Linda said I should have hair like those black girls that anchor the morning news shows. It took some effort, but it was worth it.

I made plans to return to Wilmington. The day I left Knoxville, I weighed 144 pounds—almost ninety pounds less than before the accident.

A formal New Year's Eve party for students was scheduled in the gymnasium at Wilmington High. "Everybody" would be there. The perfect time to see my classmates. And let them see me.

I selected a clingy white dress and spike heels. The dress was tasteful, but revealed two inches of bosom. I had passed my seventeenth birthday and drove to the party in a red 1957 Ford Thunderbird convertible, the kind of car that guys drool over.

The party began at 9, but I didn't get there until 10:30. I flashed a smile as everyone turned to gawk.

I saw Ben Underwood, star of the basketball team, motion for his black friends to look at the girl in the white dress. I pretended not to be paying attention to their conversation as Ben and the guys all began talking at once:

"Who the hell is that?"

"That, pal, is the girl of my dreams."

"Yeah, well, she will have the starring role in my dream tonight."

"Careful guys, you're talking about the girl I'm gonna marry."

"You're too late. I proposed to her last night."

"Yeah, r-r-right. Did your proposal include marriage?"

"Not really. There are so many girls, and I have to be fair with them. You know, spread myself around. Give 'em all a break."
"You're right. You're too much for one girl."

"I'm glad you understand."

"Does anybody know her name?"

"Does it matter?"

"Right again. Who cares if she even has a name?"

"Lord, look at those legs. And ta-ta's to die for."

"Sorry guys, she's crazy about me."

"Like hell, she is."

"Aw, you're just jealous."

The conversation trailed off as the school principal approached the boys. Mrs. Pawley had the answer to their question. "My goodness, I think that girl is Latisha Johnson. She's beautiful."

I loved the attention. Then I scanned the room before glancing back at the boys. One uncomfortable thought came to my mind, Shallow.

DERON LEE

1974

WINSTON-SALEM, NORTH CAROLINA

"Nothing greases the skids of life like money, or an old truck."

My friend's words stuck in my mind for thirty years. Since I had found money to be an elusive lubricant, I went in search of an old hauler. I wanted to take a truck to the special interest auto shows where I had met some unforgettable characters.

I examined about a dozen enduring Fords, Chevys and Dodges before I found the perfect pickup, a 1966 Ford F-100 standard short bed. A few parts were missing, but the truck had not a speck of rust. It was love at first sight, and the owner knew it. The rascal got his price, and I drove away with a special vehicle. A man in Rural Hall agreed to restore the Ford to like-new condition. Six months later, and way over budget, I had my "new" truck.

During winter months the local Ford dealership displayed my baby blue pickup in their showroom right alongside brand new vehicles. In the summer, I drove my prize possession to shows within a hundred-mile radius of my home.

At the Thursday Night Car and Truck Show in High Point, I parked my truck next to a 1946 Mercury sedan with suicide doors. The car had a For Sale sign on the windshield.

1946 Mercury, all original with 24,000 actual miles, $17,000 or best offer.

The owner was a pleasant chap in his mid-forties. He explained that the car sold new in Greensboro sixty years ago. The original owner died in 1948 and his widow kept the car in her garage for about twenty-five years until she passed away. A son took possession of the Mercury and moved it to his garage where it languished for another twenty years. From 1991 until 2005, the automobile had three owners. The current possessor had bought the black sedan one year ago. He proudly produced the original bill of sale dated February 2, 1946.

I asked, "Why are you selling your car so soon after acquiring it?"

"Lost my job. We need money. My family loves that old Mercury, but a man has to do some things he doesn't want to do."

The fellow told me he had been a security guard at High Point University for twenty-two years. "Worked my way up from guard to Chief of Security."

"What happened?"

"They got a new president, and she eliminated my position. She let my best friend go at the same time. One day, everything was all right in my world, and then I had big problems. But God will see us through this time of trouble."

A worn Bible lay open on the back seat of the Mercury. We talked a few minutes about his car, my truck, and the uncertainties of life. I wished him good luck and moved on to view more vehicles.

When I returned to my lawn chair beside my truck, a man approached me eager to talk about my Ford. He said that his brother had one just like it, except the old truck was a bucket of rust and refused to start.

"He won't get rid of that truck. He loves it. That's good, ain't it?"

"Yes, that's good."

My response opened a door for him to get chatty. "The truck used to belong to my uncle. Well, he was Ed's uncle too. Ed, that's my brother. Our uncle died a few years ago. He lived over in Winston-Salem. Do you know where Vargrave Street is in old Winston? It's just off Highway 52. Uncle Albert had the big white house that sits back off the road. You know the one?"

Winston-Salem is a city of 300,000 people. I was not sure about the location of Vargrave Street, much less his uncle's old house. The man gave me directions to the home from several points around town. In desperation, I finally agreed I knew precisely the exact house that belonged to his uncle. "The white one," I said.

"That's it! That's the one."

He was not through with me. "I'm seventy years old. Did you know that?"

"No."

"That's good, ain't it?"

"Yes."

"I had prostate cancer four years ago. I'm doing great. That's good, ain't it?"

He was not content with my smiling, mute reply. The man looked me straight in the eyes and waited for my answer.

"Yes, that's really good."

"I don't even have to go back to the doctor until next October. I think it's the twelfth of October, or maybe it's the fifteenth, my wife wrote it down somewhere."

I liked the guy. He was a happy man. But I didn't want to get into a prolonged discussion of where his wife might have misplaced the note about his doctor's appointment. I shook his hand, wished him well, and sauntered up and down the lines of cars and trucks before heading back to my truck.

A bone-thin man in his forties greeted me. His face had the red, weathered look of a guy who worked hard and drank harder. A boy, about the age of twelve, stood beside him with a hand on his dad's arm. The boy was blind.

The man talked enthusiastically about my truck. A few years ago, he had one almost like it. He told his son that the truck was a beautiful blue color, the prettiest blue he had ever seen. He continued to reel off details about the dashboard, the bed and the interior. The boy groped a hand around the headlights and along the grill.

I was trying to think of something appropriate to say when the fellow spied a 1957 Chevrolet Bel-Air in perfect condition. He scurried away from me and headed straight for the Chevy with his son shuffling along beside him. "Hey man, you take care of that truck."

I pulled my chair into a circle of car-crazy folks. We reminisced about the days gone by when cars were cars, and not look-alike jelly beans.

A lovely natural blond about eighteen years old approached us with an armful of papers. She nodded a cheerful greeting. "Ee's a question-nar-ie. Ee's for you. Please easy."

The girl captivated a teenage boy seated next to me. He asked, "Where are you from?"

"Ee's Estonia. We... me... I...am exchange student, you see."

"That's funny. You don't talk like a girl from Gastonia."

We laughed at the reference to the small town near Charlotte.

"Ee's not Gastonia. Ee's Estonia. Ee's near Finland. Do you know Finland?"

"Is that anywhere near Walnut Cove?"

More knee-slapping laughter.

"Ee's not Walnut Curve or whatever you say. Ee' s Estonia."

"You don't say. Well, I still think you talk funny for a girl from Gastonia."

128

"Ee's not true! Es' s not Gastonia."

"You mean you're not from Gastonia?"

"Yes."

"Do you mean yes, you're not from Gastonia, or yes, you are from Gastonia?"

"No, no, no, not from Gastonia."

"Well then, you shouldn't say it, if it's not true."

The delightful girl looked at my good-old-boy friend as if to say, "You poor fool."

"Ee thinks you not smart man."

"Well, I think you are smart and sooo good-looking. I'm just having a little fun with you. Guys like to tease pretty girls."

"Yes, in my country, too."

She handed out the questionnaires and we began filling in the blanks. A minute later, the young man said he needed some clarification about one of the questions. "It asks about family size."

"Yes, ee's question number four."

"Well, we are all big people. Even Mom is a big woman."

This time the laughter was riotous. She suspected he was trying to pull her leg again, but she made an attempt at explanation.

"Ee's asking how many in your family.

"I told you. All of us. We're all big people."

The beauty from the Estonia laughed along with everyone. She was not about to fall into another circle of conversation with a country boy doing his best to flirt.

She asked, "Does anyone know zee owner of zat beauteous blue truck?"

I glanced over at the young man. "You need to get yourself a truck, boy. It will grease your way through life, and someday help you find a wife."

DONALD LEE

1976

FORSYTH COUNTY, NORTH CAROLINA

"Hurry up, Don, this rehearsal is going to be special."

"I'm almost ready. It's this darn tie. It looks like a bib."

"Your tie looks fine. " Eleanor checked her watch for the umpteenth time. "Please hurry. I want to talk to the music director before services begin."

I was an ardent, if less than gifted, singer. My deep voice rumbled up my 6'6" frame. I took a back seat to my wife's lilting soprano voice.

I gave my tie a final yank. "I'm ready, let's go."

In the car Eleanor chatted about plans for the choir to sing in missions, hospitals, and an orphanage. "They say it is a lovely place, and we'll have such fun."

"I haven't seen you so happy in a long time," I said. We're going to have an adventure, but it is going to be expensive. It's a long way from North Carolina to Ecuador."

Five days later, we met Ester Schlechte, a missionary, at the Quito airport in Ecuador. After settling into our quarters, we convened in the austere lobby of our hotel. Ms. Schlechte gave a brief, lively history of the country. "We grow more bananas than any place in the world. But we have our problems. The population is divided into the Have's and Have Nots with almost no middle class as you have in America. The native Indiana form 25% of the population and are in the Have Not category. When we visit an orphanage in Esmeraldas, you will see what I mean."

It was a bumpy two-day bus ride to Esmeraldas on the Pacific coast. On the way we sang at two hospitals and a missionary post. Everywhere along the route were signs of the export of petroleum and natural gas piped in from the eastern slopes of the Andes. The rough-and-tumble docks of Esmeraldas contrasted with the serene beauty of the ocean.

The bus finally rambled into a dusty yard in front of the Displaced Children's Home. The portly, balding superintendent delivered a welcoming speech that included references to the problems of overcrowding in the dilapidated facility. We took our positions in the courtyard. Colorfully dressed children filed in and sat on the bare ground.

Eleanor nudged me and pointed to a girl about three-years-old who was dragging a threadbare canvas bag. A doll in the child's image seemed to be watching the proceedings from the rim of the bag. Then her owner lifted the doll out of the bag and propped her up for a better view of the singers. The little girl arranged the doll's dress and then glanced at Eleanor.

Eleanor gasped, "Such innocence, such beauty, and such a desperate environment".

Following the music, the children were treated to cookies and tea. Eleanor grabbed my arm. "We must meet the girl with the canvas bag. She's adorable."

I allowed myself to be pulled along until we came face to face with Joan, who had been given an English name by officials at the orphanage.

Eleanor asked, "What's your doll's name?"

Joan said nothing but held up her doll for a closer inspection. Eleanor bent down and touched the doll's flowing black hair and faded white dress. Joan beamed.

The shy little girl was all Eleanor could talk about that day and night. Gradually, she introduced the idea of adoption.

I said, "You've got to be crazy. We can't afford it. We're too old. The officials would never permit a black family to adopt. "

"You don't have to tell me we don't have a lot of money or remind me of our ages, Don Lee."

The next day Eleanor seemed reconciled to leaving Joan behind. However, I made some inquiries about the process of adoption. The superintendent told me that in order to be eligible for adoption a child must be either abandoned or orphaned. "In the case of Joan, Mr. Lee, her fourteen- year-old mother could not care for her. We sometimes release a child to the custody of prospective parents, but the Tribunal de Menores must grant permission. The process is routine and can be accomplished quickly for a few American dollars. It is even possible that you and Mrs. Lee could leave Ecuador with Joan, but the adoption would not be final until it is processed through a U.S. based adoption agency authorized to deal with Ecuadorian officials."

We made a final visit to the orphanage with several gifts for Joan. Eleanor wanted to assure Joan that more presents would follow on her birthday and Christmas, and every birthday and Christmas thereafter.

Joan had been told that we were coming by with gifts and some good news. When she emerged from a doorway, Joan was dragging her battered canvas bag. The bag appeared to be heavier than before, and she pulled it along with both hands. She greeted us with a brilliant smile.

"What's in the bag, sweetheart?" Eleanor asked.

The superintendent repeated, "Que es en el bolsillo?"

Joan pulled her doll from the bag, and then removed the contents one by one. Two dresses, one pair of shoes, six pairs of underwear, three pair of socks, a toothbrush, and a comb. Except for the clothes she was wearing, it was everything Joan had it the world.

Eleanor and I stared at the articles with our mouths agape. Joan had come prepared to leave the orphanage and go with us to our home in a mysterious land.

Tears welled in Eleanor's eyes and spilled down her cheeks. She looked up at me. I ushered her to a corner of the courtyard where we could talk privately.

"Don, before you start, I'm sorry I cried, but I couldn't help it. I know we can't take her with us, but you are going to have to tell her. I can't do it."

"Tell her what? I'm not going to tell that little girl anything except that she is going with us. Did you see the look in her eyes? We can't let her down."

"But, Don, can we afford it? It won't be easy."

"Life isn't easy. We can pinch pennies, and she will be a lot better off than she would staying here."

"What will the kids think?"

"Our boys have big hearts, and they will love their little sister. We're taking her home. Our sweet Joan is going to be a Lee."

CPSIA information can be obtained
at www.ICGtesting.com
Printed in the USA
LVOW04s1532230616
493838LV00019B/946/P

AUG 1 0 2016

9 781630 661885